PRAISE FOR DONNA GRANT'S BESTSELLING ROMANCE NOVELS

"Time travel, ancient legends, and seductive romance are seamlessly interwoven into one captivating package."

–*Publishers Weekly* on Midnight's Master

"Dark, sexy, magical. When I want to indulge in a sizzling fantasy adventure, I read Donna Grant."

–Allison Brennan, *New York Times* bestseller

5 Stars! Top Pick! "An absolute must read! From beginning to end, it's an incredible ride."

–*Night Owl Reviews*

"It's good vs. evil Druid in the next installment of Grant's Dark Warrior series. The stakes get higher as discerning one's true loyalties become harder. Grant's compelling characters and continued presence of previous protagonists are key reasons why these books are so gripping. Another exciting and thrilling chapter!"

–*RT Book Reviews* on Midnight's Lover

"Donna Grant has given the paranormal genre a burst of fresh air..."

–*San Francisco Book Review*

DON'T MISS THESE OTHER SPELLBINDING NOVELS BY NYT & USA TODAY BESTSELLING AUTHOR DONNA GRANT

Contemporary Paranormal

THE SKYE DRUIDS

(Spin off series from the *Reaper* series, as well as the *Dark Kings, Dragon Kings, Dark Warriors*, and *Dark Sword*)

Iron Ember

Shoulder the Sky

* * *

DRAGON KINGS

(Spin off series from *Dark Kings*)

Dragon Revealed (novella)

Dragon Mine

Dragon Unbound (novella)

Dragon Eternal

Dragon Lover (novella)

* * *

REAPER SERIES

Dark Alpha's Claim

Dark Alpha's Embrace

Dark Alpha's Demand

Dark Alpha's Lover

Tall Dark Deadly Alpha Bundle

Dark Alpha's Night

Dark Alpha's Awakening

Dark Alpha's Redemption

Dark Alpha's Temptation

Dark Alpha's Caress

Dark Alpha's Obsession

Dark Alpha's Need

Dark Alpha's Silent Night

Dark Alpha's Passion

Dark Alpha's Command

Dark Alpha's Fury

DARK KINGS

Dark Heat (3 novella compilation)

Darkest Flame

Fire Rising

Burning Desire

Hot Blooded

Night's Blaze

Soul Scorched

Dragon King (novella)

Passion Ignites

Smoldering Hunger

Smoke and Fire

Dragon Fever (novella)

Firestorm

Blaze

Dragon Burn (novella)

Constantine: A History (short story)

Heat

Torched

Dragon Night (novella)

Dragonfire

Dragon Claimed (novella)

Ignite

Fever

Dragon Lost (novella)

Flame

Inferno

Whisky and Wishes (novella)

Heart of Gold

Of Fire and Flame (novella)

* * *

DARK WARRIORS

Midnight's Master

Midnight's Lover

Midnight's Seduction

Midnight's Warrior

Midnight's Kiss

Midnight's Captive

Midnight's Temptation

Midnight's Promise

Midnight's Surrender (novella)

A Warrior for Christmas

Dark Warrior Box Set

* * *

CHIASSON SERIES

Wild Fever

Wild Dream

Wild Need

Wild Flame

Wild Rapture

* * *

LARUE SERIES

Moon Kissed

Moon Thrall

Moon Struck

Moon Bound

* * *

Historical Paranormal

THE KINDRED

Everkin

Eversong

Everwylde

Everbound

Evernight

Everspell

* * *

KINDRED: THE FATED

(Spin off series from the *Kindred*)

Rage

Ruin

Reign

* * *

DARK SWORD

Dangerous Highlander

Forbidden Highlander

Wicked Highlander

Untamed Highlander

Shadow Highlander

Darkest Highlander

Dark Sword Box Set

* * *

ROGUES OF SCOTLAND

The Craving

The Hunger

The Tempted

The Seduced

Rogues of Scotland Box Set

* * *

THE SHIELDS

A Dark Guardian

A Kind of Magic

A Dark Seduction

A Forbidden Temptation

A Warrior's Heart

Mystic Trinity (connected)

* * *

DRUIDS GLEN

Highland Mist

Highland Nights

Highland Dawn

Highland Fires

Highland Magic

Mystic Trinity (connected)

SISTERS OF MAGIC

Shadow Magic

Echoes of Magic

Dangerous Magic

Sisters of Magic Boxed Set

THE ROYAL CHRONICLES NOVELLA SERIES

Prince of Desire

Prince of Seduction

Prince of Love

Prince of Passion

Royal Chronicles Box Set

Mystic Trinity (connected)

* * *

Military Romance / Romantic Suspense

SONS OF TEXAS

The Hero

The Protector

The Legend

The Defender

The Guardian

* * *

Cowboy / Contemporary

HEART OF TEXAS SERIES

The Christmas Cowboy Hero

Cowboy, Cross My Heart

My Favorite Cowboy

A Cowboy Like You

Looking for a Cowboy

A Cowboy Kind of Love

* * *

STAND ALONE BOOKS

Home for a Cowboy Christmas

Mutual Desire

Forever Mine

Savage Moon

* * *

Dark Beginnings: A First in Series Boxset

Contains:

Chiasson Series, Book 1: Wild Fever

LaRue Series, Book 1: Moon Kissed

The Royal Chronicles Series, Book 1: Prince of Desire

Check out Donna Grant's Online Store, www.donnagrant.com/shop, for autographed books, character themed goodies, and more!

HIGHLAND MAGIC

A DRUIDS GLEN NOVEL

DONNA GRANT

HIGHLAND MAGIC

ISBN 13: 978-1-942017-31-8
Available in ebook and print editions

www.DonnaGrant.com
www.MotherofDragonsBooks.com

ACKNOWLEDGMENTS

There's no way I could do any of this without my amazing kiddos–Gillian and Connor–thanks for putting up with my hectic schedule and for knowing when it was time that I got out of the house for a spell. And special nod to the Grant pets–Sheba, Sassy, Diego, and Sisko–who love to walk on the keyboard or demand some loving regardless of what I'm doing.

Last but not least, my readers. You have my eternal gratitude for the amazing support you show me and my books. Y'all rock my world. Enjoy!

xoxox

DG

1

Lorem Northwestern Scotland
Fall 1625

For as long as he could remember, Frang had yearned to rid himself of the curse that made him immortal, standing guard at the Druids Glen and leading the Druids. How many years had passed since he'd stood in the midst of the peaceful magical stones of the Druids Glen?

Too many.

And it didn't matter anymore. He'd left his stones, though they weren't really his. He had guarded the Druids as he could with the help of the lairds of MacInnes.

Frang ran a hand down his face and sighed loudly. Countless people he'd watched die, many before their time. He had seen love lost and love found, foes vanquished and even seen the enemy invade a castle to kill innocent children.

Yet, it was all in the past now.

He looked down into the waters of the lake at his

reflection. He had gotten used to seeing the long white hair and beard. It seemed rather...odd...that he looked again as he had that fateful day over three hundred years before.

Frang sat back on his heels and glanced over his shoulder. His need to return to the Glen was strong. With the prophecy finished, he was no longer needed, but it didn't matter. He could return now. No one would recognize him. But he knew it wasn't just wishful thinking. His time at the Druids Glen was over. He needed to accept that.

A soft movement filled the air. It was the only thing that alerted him he was no longer alone. Slowly, Frang rose and turned to face his long-time friend.

"Aimery," he said with a welcoming smile.

The Fae commander returned the smile and held out his arm. After they'd clasped forearms, Aimery stepped back and looked him up and down. "It will take some time for me to get used to this appearance again."

Frang laughed as he raked his hands through his hair and glanced over the impeccably dressed Fae. Aimery's long flaxen hair was held away from his face by several rows of tiny intricate braids that would have looked feminine on anyone else but him.

"The first thing I did was shave the beard." Frang scratched his bare chin absently. "It has been on my face so long my skin doesn't know what to do."

"It won't take long." Aimery clapped him on the back and smiled as they sat on a fallen tree. "What are your plans?"

Frang shrugged and looked toward the still waters of

the lake. "I don't really know. The Druids were my life, even before the curse. What can I do now?"

"You get to start over," Aimery said after a short silence. "Do anything you want, become anyone you want. Not many get that chance."

"I like who I am," Frang argued. "I am a Druid High Priest who knows more about the Fae and the Druids than any human in this realm."

Aimery's swirling blue eyes met his. The Fae's gaze was intense, never wavering as he peered deep into Frang's soul.

There was no doubt that Aimery was looking into his future. The longer he stared, the more worried Frang became. "What do you see?" he asked softly.

Aimery blinked and turned away. "I'm not in the habit of telling someone their future."

"I'm not just someone," Frang reminded him.

With a loud sigh Aimery turned his fair head until his gaze returned to Frang. "You don't want to know your future, my friend. No one ever really does. Live this new life you've been granted, and don't look back."

Frang swallowed and stood to pace the edge of the lake. "There are only two reasons you wouldn't tell me my future. One possibility is that I'm going to die very soon. The second is that I'm going to have to make a very difficult choice and by telling me the future you'll influence me."

He turned to look at the Fae commander only to find Aimery grinning. "I taught you well," Aimery said with a nod. "You'll do fine, Frang."

And with that, Aimery was gone.

For several long moments Frang stared at the log and where Aimery had sat. Decade after decade he had given to the Druids and the Fae, giving his blood as well as his soul all because of one stupid, reckless night that had cursed him for three hundred years.

He looked down at the robes that had been his daily wear as the Druid High Priest. They would only serve to draw attention to him, something he wanted to avoid at all costs. With a sigh, he turned toward the road that would take him to the nearest village where he could buy some new clothes.

"And a new life," he muttered as he slapped his hand on his leg in agitation of the unknown.

He promptly noticed the clothes neatly folded on the log. Frang didn't have to wonder if they fit. He knew they would.

"Thank you, Aimery," he said as he reached for the garments.

With one final glance at his Druid robes, he pulled them over his head. After a quick wash in the loch, he returned to the log and reached for Aimery's gift.

Frang had to admit he liked his new clothes. He looked down at the saffron shirt and bold blue and green plaid with red and orange accents. It was a plaid he knew well, very well. The tall boots were made of supple leather that fit his feet and legs to perfection, and the brooch holding his plaid was made of silver and held the crest of the Fae, a dragon head with intricate knot work surrounding it.

There was only one thing left. The sword.

It had been three hundred years since he had last held a sword. He lifted it and held it in both hands as he looked over the weapon.

A more beautiful sword Frang had never seen. The

pommel was fluted and fit his hand flawlessly. The cross guards and pommel were adorned with the same intricate and beautiful knots that decorated his brooch.

Slowly, he pulled the sword from its scabbard. The weight of the weapon was as near to perfect as it could get. Frang stared in awe at the blade where the Fae symbol had been added, and surrounding it was even more of the knot work he had come to love.

He lunged and swung the sword around him, testing its weight as he tested himself. By the time he was satisfied, sweat soaked his shirt and ran down his face. Frang returned the weapon to its sheath with a smile. After he folded his Druid robes and left them on the log, he picked up his sword and slung the strap over his head, so the scabbard settled between his shoulder blades.

With a sigh, he turned to face his future. No longer was he a Druid, but a warrior.

2

Northern Scotland, Clan Wallace
April, five years later

Kenna pushed her hair away from her face as she rose to her feet and grabbed the basket of herbs she had been gathering.

She blew a curl that had fallen from her braid out of her face and sighed loudly. Her back ached from bending over all morning. She looked down at the small amount of herbs she had gathered and knew it would be awhile yet before she returned to her cottage.

With her gaze searching the ground for linden, which was becoming more difficult to find, she moved deftly through the underbrush of the forest. More and more people came to her for amulets to ward off evil, for love potions, or cures for their illnesses. It was just a matter of time before the Wallace discovered what she really was. A Druid.

For years she had kept her secret, but she feared that

secret was no longer safe. Once the Wallace found her out, it meant either her death...or slavery.

The Wallace was a hard man and a powerful laird. He gave no quarter and expected none in return. The few times she had been called to the castle, she'd had to make herself appear relaxed instead of running out of the gates and never looking back. Yet, his attention had turned to her, making him visit her more often than she'd like.

Kenna sighed again. There was no linden to be found. She would have to return home and look for more on the morrow. Her eyes moved about the forest. Walking amid the tall pines and sturdy oaks was something she greatly enjoyed.

But today, she couldn't find the peace that normally filled her. Something was wrong. She closed her eyes and concentrated on her surroundings as she tried to determine what had unbalanced around her.

No matter how hard she concentrated, the answer stayed just out of her reach. Farther and farther into herself she went until she saw a flash of a brooch with a dragon head on it and ancient knot work surrounding it. Kenna's eyes flew open, and she leaned against an oak as she tried to put her breathing back to normal. The brooch was a sign, but of what? Evil coming her way? Or maybe someone to aid in her Druid teaching?

She shook her head and pushed away from the tree. She would get no answers in the forest. How she wished Brigit was still alive to teach her more of the Druid ways. It had been Brigit who had trained her to be the midwife and healer of the Wallace clan. Because Kenna lived close to the border between the Wallaces and Carmichaels, she helped both clans when needed, since healers were hard to come by.

A smile pulled at her lips as she began her journey back to her cottage. Thoughts of Brigit always made her smile. Brigit had been a strong force as a woman. Everyone had respected her and sought her out on many occasions.

The sudden cry of pheasants as they took to the air alerted Kenna that she wasn't alone. She didn't slow her steps, though her heart pounded like a drum in her ears. Normally she stayed off the road that went through the forest, but today she was glad it was only a little ways ahead of her.

She had to fight the urge to run when she heard a twig snap behind her. The need to turn around and face her pursuer was strong, but she made herself continue as if she didn't know she was being followed.

When she saw the road through the branches, she gripped her basket tighter and reached for the dirk hidden inside beneath the herbs. If she didn't find help on the road, she would have to face her attacker because she couldn't outrun him.

No sooner had she stepped out of the forest than she heard a deep voice behind her say, "Look what we have here, men. A tasty morsel ta be sure."

Kenna slowly turned to face the man and blanched when she saw two others emerge from behind him. She glanced at their tartan and noticed the blue and green plaid of the Carmichaels.

"May I help you?" she asked, hoping they didn't hear the fear in her voice.

The man in the middle, obviously the leader, stepped

forward and looked her over with his black eyes. "Ye can remove yer clothes."

Kenna took a deep breath and kept her grip on the dirk. Though she had helped the Carmichaels in the past, not many knew who she was. "You are on Wallace land."

"We ken where we're at," said the red headed man on the right. He was missing several teeth and sported a nasty scar that mangled his left ear and half of his face.

She took a tentative step back and wondered where the patrol was. The Wallace always had men patrolling the border.

"You would be wise to leave me be. I am Kenna Frasier, healer to the Wallace clan."

The leader let out a bark of laughter. "We wouldna care if ye were the Wallace's daughter. We'll take what we want. Ken?"

"You will bring about a war," she warned, but it was too late. The men were already advancing on her.

Frang slowly unsheathed his sword as he watched the scene with the woman and three men unfold. He looked over each man, noticing any weaknesses.

Slowly, he crept out of the forest, keeping his gaze on the men at all times. He was halfway to the men before the one on the woman's left, a man with stringy blond hair, turned and saw him.

"We've got company," he shouted to his companions as he drew his sword.

Frang stopped and prepared for the attack. The blond reached him first. He raised his sword as the blond swung his blade down toward Frang's head. Out of the corner of his eye, he saw the leader of the men advance on the woman, but Frang knew he'd never reach her in time. He could only hope she'd run as soon as she got the chance.

Pain ripped through his left arm. He staggered back and touched his arm only to come away with blood on his fingers. He looked from his fingers to his attacker. It had been many years since Frang had seen his own blood.

He pushed aside the pain and gripped his sword as he took a step toward the blond. Instinct took over as the man charged him. Frang didn't think, only reacted. Their swords clanged again and again as Frang blocked each attempt as the blond tried to kill him.

Frang knew the moment he let down his guard the blond would succeed. There was no way Frang had lived three hundred years with a curse only to die a few years later. He growled as he spun on his foot and swung his sword with all his might. He heard a gurgling sound and saw his blade sticking in the blond's side.

Frang pulled his weapon free as soon as he heard footsteps coming toward him. He turned just in time to block a swing that was meant to sever his head from his body. This time he faced the red-headed giant whose every swing of his sword came harder and harder.

The giant might be stronger, but Frang was quicker. He used his agility to dodge blows that would have knocked him to the ground. The giant was clumsy, and Frang easily sidestepped each of his swings, saving Frang's strength.

With a roar, the giant raised his sword over his head. Frang saw his chance and lunged forward as his blade sunk into the giant's chest. The giant's eyes bulged before his arms dropped and he fell to the ground.

Frang took a deep breath as he pulled the sword from

the giant. All that was left was the leader. A glance told Frang the woman had vanished. At least she was safe.

"'Tisna yer fight," the leader said, his eyes holding a measure of fear now that his two comrades were dead.

Frang shrugged as he walked toward the leader. "You made it my fight when you decided to attack a woman."

"We only wanted some fun."

Frang licked his lips. "Then I'd say you picked the wrong woman to have fun with. Ken?"

The leader looked to his fallen comrades before he turned on his heel and ran back into the forest. Frang sighed and let the tip of his sword touch the ground. He leaned on it and turned to look at his bloodied arm.

He needed to get it cleaned and find some herbs to put on it before it became infected. His gaze followed the blade of his sword and the knot work etched on it as he watched the blood run down to puddle on the packed earth.

"You need to tend to that wound."

Frang jerked and spun around to find the woman standing behind him. His gaze fixed on her amazing flame red hair that hung in one thick braid over her shoulder. Several strands had come loose and hung in soft curls around her enticing oval face. Her large eyes stared at him, never wavering. Brows that were only slightly darker than her hair gently arched over her eyes. Her nose was small and delicate, and her lips full and wide.

Frang cleared his throat as he let his gaze slide down the rest of her, lush curves and all. It had been a long time since he had looked at a woman to fill his bed.

"Aye, mistress. You shouldn't be out here alone," he

said. He withdrew the sword, inspected it and wiped it off on the tunic on one of the dead men before he sheathed it.

The woman continued to stare at him. "I'm always alone," she finally said.

He liked the sound of her voice. It was soft and seductive. He closed his eyes and sighed. He couldn't last remember a time when just the sound of a women's voice made him lusty.

"Come," the woman said. "I will tend to your wound."

Frang opened his eyes. "Thank you, but nay. I need to be on my way."

She cocked a hand on her hip while the other held her basket in the crook of her arm. "I am a healer, sir. It is what I do. Now, let me repay you for your gallantry."

Frang knew he ought to refuse. After all, he knew exactly what herbs he needed to staunch the flow of blood and speed the healing. Yet, the need to feel a woman's hands on him was strong. For far too long he had seen to other's needs. Maybe it was time he let someone see to his.

"All right."

She smiled and turned into the forest. Frang quickly followed her, noting she was going the way he had just come. After the years of travelling he'd done, what was another day?

By the time they reached her cottage, Frang welcomed the peace of her home. His arm had begun to ache, and the bleeding had intensified. All he wanted to do was eat a hot meal and sleep.

Yet, he pushed all that aside as he kept his senses alert as they walked to the door to her small cottage. The structure itself was nestled deep in the forest, surrounded by tall pines with clusters of ferns on the ground. It was a peaceful setting, one that seemed to compliment the woman.

She opened the door and motioned him to the table. Frang wearily sank into a chair. After she set aside her basket he watched as she moved about the cottage collecting leaves from plants hanging from the beams of the ceiling.

Her movements were graceful but quick, sometimes she didn't even look up at the plant she reached for. Frang held back a smile as she absently brushed a lock of hair behind her ear.

He sat forward when she moved aside a piece of fabric separating the main cottage from another room. At first, he thought it might be where she slept, but after spotting her bed across from the hearth realized the room most likely was where she mixed her herbs.

When he heard her begin to hum, he leaned his head back on the chair and closed his eyes. He smelled cinnamon and let out a deep breath. It was as if he were still in the Glen. A longing for the magic and peace of the Glen ran through him so swift and true, it nearly doubled him over.

A soft hand touched his face and Frang found himself leaning against it.

"Does the wound ache?"

He opened his eyes to look at the woman above him. Her eyes were the most beautiful things he had ever seen. Their color was that of the sky at sunset, a magnificent amber color. Mystical. Seductive. Beautiful.

Frang swallowed and made himself look away. "Nay. The tenderness of the wound is minimal."

"They why did you look as though you were in great pain?"

Frang grinned and sat up, hating when her hand dropped from his face. "Memories tend to do that at times."

She took a step away from him and clasped her hands at her waist. "My apologies, sir."

"Frang," he corrected her. "My name is Frang."

The corners of her mouth tilted up slightly. "It is good to meet you, Frang. I am Kenna."

3

Kenna had to clasp her hands together to keep from touching the stranger who had saved her. He was handsome enough with his wide shoulders and muscular arms. His jaw was strong, his lips thin. She longed to run her hands through his shoulder-length light brown hair streaked with golden highlights.

But it was his eyes that held her captive. One glimpse into his sky-blue eyes and she had glimpsed an old soul, a soul that had seen and suffered much.

"The herbs are nearly done," Kenna said to break the silence.

He unsettled her, something no one had done before. She looked around her cottage and spotted lemon balm hanging near the hearth. She reached for one of the leaves and then moved to Frang's sword. As soon as her hand touched the hilt, his covered hers.

She raised her gaze to look into his bright blue eyes. "'Tis but lemon balm. Attached to your sword, it will staunch any blood."

After a moment he released her hand, and she tied the herbs around the base of the hilt near the pommel where it would not get in his way. She stood and stepped back. She wasn't sure why she had given him the lemon balm. Never before had she given it to someone for their weapon.

"Thank you," he said softly.

She nodded and turned to enter her backroom. After grinding a few more herbs together to make a fine powder, she set the bowl aside and reached for some cloth. The Adder's Tongue, one of her special herbs that had been soaking in water, was ready. She pulled it out and placed it on the cloth.

She gathered the cloth and the bowl then went back to Frang who sat with his head, once again, leaning back on the chair. He watched her closely as she approached. He stared at her as no one else ever had, with a hint of something deeper in gaze, something that made her stomach flutter and her blood heat. A strange emotion unfurled low in her belly, and the need to touch him, to feel his warmth was more than she could deny herself.

Silently, Kenna knelt beside the chair and reached to move aside his torn shirt, but before she could, he reached up and unpinned the brooch that held his plaid to let the tartan fall to his waist. Then he pulled his shirt over his head and leaned back.

Kenna took a deep breath and tried not to stare at the expanse of muscular chest and stomach that rippled with muscles. She had seen many a man without their shirts, but Frang was the first who made her want to run her hands over him at her leisure.

Her hand shook as she reached for the cloth. As gently

as she could, she used the cloth to wipe away the blood and make sure the wound was cleaned. Once that was finished, she sprinkled the herb powder into the cut. Then, she took the cloth with the soaked Adder's Tongue and placed it over the wound and tied it in place.

With no other excuse to touch him, she rose and inspected her handiwork. "Would you like something to drink?"

He nodded and eagerly drank the water she gave him. Afterwards, he closed his eyes. For long moments she stared at him until his breathing evened into sleep. Only then did she turn and enter her backroom to work.

Frang took a deep breath and gradually came awake. The pain in his arm had abated for the most part. He raised his arm and moved it about to test it.

"Already you pull at the wound."

He turned his head at the sound of Kenna's voice. She stood in the doorway of her backroom and watched him. He rose and reached for his torn and bloodied shirt.

"I will be careful."

"It needs to be stitched."

He stopped mid-motion and looked at her. "I've taken enough of your time."

One shoulder lifted in a shrug. "What will be a waste of time is if you walk from my cottage now and reopen your wound during another fight. If you're going to leave now let me stitch it."

Frang lowered his shirt. "I don't go looking for fights."

"Be that as it may, this is Scotland. You aren't a Wallace. That in itself could cause bloodshed."

"As you wish," he said as he sat back down.

His gaze followed her as she collected a needle and thread and more herbs before she returned to him. He wanted more of her soft touch. Her hands soothed him more than the herbs. The way she had smoothed her hands over his skin had made him want to pull her against his chest and ravage her mouth with a kiss that would leave her breathless and aching for more of him as he was beginning to ache for her.

This time she pulled the other chair around the table and sat. She untied the bandage and removed the Adder's Tongue with the cloth.

"Already it looks better," she murmured.

Frang's gaze never left her face. She was serious about her healing, and it made him wonder how she would fit in at the Druid's Glen. With a little training she could very well be a Druid. Anyone with healing talents like hers was greatly sought after.

"You have a gentle touch," he said as she threaded the needle.

She glanced at him, a slight grin on her lips. "A healer with rough hands is worthless."

"True enough. Who trained you?"

She paused for just a heartbeat, but it was enough to tell him she was cautious, which made him wonder if she would tell him the truth.

"An old woman in my clan. She had no children to pass on her knowledge. When it became apparent I had some skill, she showed me the way."

He was more than curious now. "I think I'd like to meet her."

Kenna turned to him with needle in hand. "That would be difficult since she died five winters back."

"I'm sorry."

"Don't be," she said as she leaned close to his arm, her warm breath fanning his skin and making his rod stir.

Frang turned his head from her and closed his eyes as his body reacted to her nearness. Just as the first prick of the needle touched his skin, the sound of approaching horses caught both of their attentions.

Kenna jumped up, her chest rising and falling rapidly. "Hide." When he didn't move, she turned to him and all but shoved him out of the chair as she threw his shirt at him. "Hide, Frang. In my backroom. Make sure you aren't seen."

Frang moved to do as she asked, though he wondered why she wanted him to hide. Who was it she feared so much? Once he was in her backroom, he pulled the curtain closed and watched her through the crack as she tossed his bandage in the hearth. She moved to the table to gather the needle and herbs when the door flew open.

4

Kenna tried to stop her knees from shaking as the imposing figure of her laird, Glenn Wallace, stepped into her cottage.

He was young and most considered him handsome with his blond hair and hazel eyes. If Kenna was anything other than a Druid, she might not fear him so.

The Wallace's gaze moved slowly around her cottage, stopping at the table where the supplies to stitch Frang's arm still lay. Kenna met his gaze and waited.

"Is anything amiss, Kenna?" he asked as he leaned against her door.

"Nay, laird. Why would you think that?"

He took a deep breath. His wide chest expanded as his muscles stretched and contracted. "I found two dead Carmichaels on the road. Do you know anything about that?"

For a moment Kenna thought about lying but knew in the end the truth was needed. "Aye, laird. I was out gathering herbs when three men, Carmichael men, stopped me."

"Three?" he asked as he pushed off the door.

She nodded. "I warned them they were on Wallace land and that I was your healer, but they didn't seem to hear. They were about to attack me when a stranger came out of the woods and stopped them."

"Stranger?" The Wallace's brow furrowed at her words. "Where is this stranger?"

Kenna shrugged. "He killed two of the men, but the third ran off instead of fighting."

"And you didn't come to report this to me?"

Kenna straightened and returned her laird's glare. "Least you forget, laird, I was nearly raped by three men. All I thought about was the safety of my cottage, and that's where I ran."

For several heartbeats, her laird stared at her. Then he crossed his arms over his chest and nodded toward the table. "And the needle and thread?"

"I may be a healer, but I also have mending to do."

Her stomach clenched so tight she worried she might double over with the fear.

"This is just another reason for you to move to the safety of the castle walls, Kenna," he said as he dropped his arms and moved closer to her.

Kenna lowered her gaze but didn't retreat as she wanted. "I prefer it here. This is my home."

"But I cannot protect you here," he argued.

She raised her gaze to his then. "I'm not asking for your protection."

"You are part of my clan, Kenna, which makes you my responsibility to protect. Why do you fight me on this?"

"It is not my intent," she said softly and glanced at his soldiers outside her door. "This is my home."

He gave a loud sigh before he reached out and touched her face with his fingertips. "Is there anything I can say to change your mind?"

Kenna shook her head.

"I will have the patrols check on you daily, then. I cannot have my healer hurt." He turned and started for the door. As he reached the doorway, he paused then turned to look at her over his shoulder. "If you ever need anything, you only need to come to me."

Kenna gave him a smile. "You are very kind, laird."

She waited until he was atop his horse and galloping away before she closed the door. No sooner had she turned to tell Frang he could come out than there was a knock at her door. Kenna opened it to find one of her clansmen needing some herbs for a stiff neck.

Kenna glanced at her backroom and prayed Frang would stay there until she went to him.

* * *

Frang lost count of the number of people who came to visit Kenna after her laird. He had been most interested in the laird of the Wallaces, and he knew just by looking at the man that he was a formidable opponent. If he was going to stay on Wallace land, he needed the laird as a friend.

He had lowered himself to the floor and watched Kenna through the crack in the curtain. The people who came to her respected her and her words. They listened raptly as she told them how to use the herbs, and he knew each of them would follow those instructions perfectly.

He leaned his head back against the wall and closed his eyes. He had no wish to leave now that darkness was descending, not to mention he found Kenna intriguing. She had so many attributes of a Druid that for a moment when she had tended his wound, he had thought she was one.

Though he longed to ask her if she had some Druid training, he suspected she would most likely lie since she didn't trust him. He was used to being trusted, used to having people seek out his advice. Leaving the Druid's Glen had been the most painful thing he had ever done. Yet, making a new life for himself was proving to be almost as painful.

No one could know he was a Druid for it would mean his death. Christians had made sure all the pagans and Druids were hanged or burned as soon as they were discovered.

Frang sighed. Aye, his life was going to be vastly different. Aimery had advised him to grasp his gift with both hands, but it was difficult when all Frang wanted to do was return to the Glen and the magical stones. Even after five years, the Glen still called to him.

He opened his hands palm up and gazed at them. For centuries, his hands had used the power of the Druids and even the powers of the Fae on occasion. How many times had he fought against the curse that bound him? Yet now he longed to have the curse returned.

His eyes closed again as he took a deep breath. Kenna's soothing voice lulled him to sleep. He yawned as he listened to her explain what the willow root was for and how the woman needed to use it.

It was the last thing he heard.

* * *

Kenna wiped her hands on her skirt as she closed the door behind her last visitor. She moved to her window and reached out to close the shutters when her gaze caught the purple sky. The sun was sinking fast in the sky.

She closed the shutters and turned to her backroom. Frang had not made a sound while she had seen to her people. Her heart began to beat wildly as she realized he might have left out her back window. She told herself it was because she was worried about his wound, but she knew it for the lie it was. In truth, she liked the way her body reacted to him, and she wanted to experience more of the heat and...desire.

As she reached to move the curtain aside her hand shook. Unhurriedly, she lifted the fabric and caught sight of his booted feet. She followed his legs until she found him leaning against the wall. Asleep.

His lips were slightly parted, and his body was relaxed. She bit her lip and knelt beside him. The deep yearning to touch him prompted her to run her fingers over his sculpted arm. Heat infused her skin. Her breath passed shakily from her lips when she found herself leaning forward to kiss him. Her lips were breaths from his when she pulled back, unable touch her lips against his.

Kenna stood on trembling legs and tried to tamp down the strange and joyous feelings running through her. She pushed aside the curtain and walked into the room to close and lock the shutters. When she turned back to Frang, his eyes were open and staring at her.

What few men had slept in her cottage had been ill. None had ever been there for any other reason, and the fact that she wanted him frightened her to the marrow of her bones. The air suddenly became thick, and it grew hard for her to breathe as she focused on Frang.

"I will leave," he said as if reading her mind.

Kenna smoothed back the hair from her face and licked her lips. Her stomach plummeted to her feet when she saw his gaze move to her mouth. Did he yearn to kiss her as she longed to feel his lips on hers? She had no experience with men, so didn't dare to ask questions she might not want to know the answer to.

"I have not stitched your wound."

He rose as nimble as a cat. "Then let us get to it."

Kenna had always known she was different, but the fact Frang wanted to spend as little time with her as necessary stung. She moved to walk past him when his arm stopped her. That simple touch made her close her eyes and force herself not to lean against him.

"You are unmarried. It isn't right that I am here alone with you."

She opened her eyes and smiled, relieved it wasn't her who made him want to leave. "Frang, I am a healer. People come in and out of my cottage at all hours of the night."

He looked into her eyes for a long moment before he nodded and released her arm. Kenna walked to her table, conscious of every move he made.

His mere presence filled her small cottage. She turned

to find him staring at her. With her hand she motioned for him to sit. She waited silently as he slowly walked to the chair and lowered himself.

Kenna flexed her fingers as she once again took the chair next to him and reached for the needle. She leaned close to him to inspect the wound and see if the herbs had begun their magic or not. And stared dumbfounded at the wound.

"What is it?" His voice held a note of concern, though it rose no higher than a whisper.

She raised her gaze to his and found herself lost in his pale blue eyes, eyes that seemed far older than he looked. She blinked and shook her head. Another glance at the wound showed her she hadn't imagined it.

The wound had begun to heal.

Before she could answer Frang, he looked down at the wound. His jaw hardened and he reached for his saffron shirt. Noting she still held the needle in her hand, Kenna lowered it to the table as she stood.

"My herbs are good, Frang. Very good. But I have never had someone heal this quickly."

He ignored her as he fastened his tartan over his heart with the brooch. Only then did he turn to look at her. "You must be better than you realized."

Kenna knew that wasn't the truth. For months now she had practiced just as Brigit had told her. Had her Druid skills finally come to her? If so, she would need to be more careful in the future least her clan hang her for a witch.

Just the thought of a noose around her neck sent chills down her spine. She wrapped her arms around her stomach and took a deep breath.

"I am just a healer."

There was something in the way Frang's blue gaze narrowed ever so slightly on her, the way his eyes seemed to search her very soul that left her frightened and...excited. It was as if he saw her secret, a secret she had kept to herself for so long. She was tired of being alone, tired of sharing her meals with only herself. Frang's sharp gaze saw her for what she was, and he accepted her.

She licked her lips and turned to the hearth. She began to pile wood inside until Frang touched her arms.

"Allow me," he said and moved her away.

It had been so long since anyone had done anything for Kenna. She was used to being alone and doing everything herself. Oh, some clansmen would trade their skills at fixing her roof or chopping wood in exchange for herbs, but that wasn't the same as doing something out of kindness.

Frang glanced over his shoulder at her and smiled. "You look as though you don't know what to do with a man in your house, lass."

A hysterical chuckled escaped before she had time to stop it. She swallowed and shrugged. "'Tis a fact, I'm afraid."

His gaze grew warm, and a slow sensual smile pulled at his wide lips. It was enough to make any woman squirm, but Kenna found her reaction alarming. She wasn't used to attention by a man, especially a man as handsome as Frang. It was obvious from the heat in his gaze that he would teach her what to do with a man in her house if she but asked. The question was, was she daring enough to ask?

"Doona fash yourself," he said as he turned back to the growing fire. "I would rather harm myself than you."

Not wanting to be caught staring at his nice bum, Kenna turned toward the area she used as her kitchen and began to make the evening meal.

"'Tis late," she said. "You are welcome to stay for dinner."

"I'd like that."

She swallowed and took a deep breath. She hadn't expected him to accept the offer, and now that he had, she found a bold side of herself she didn't know she had. "You're also welcome to stay the night."

There was a slight pause as she heard him move around the hearth toward her. She could feel his eyes on her, roaming over her body. Her skin grew flushed, her heart accelerated and breathing became difficult. She couldn't help but wonder what was going through his mind.

In fact, she was wondering what was wrong with her. She'd never invited anyone to stay the night before, especially not a strange man. Yet it seemed the right thing to do. At least, that's what her body wanted her to do.

"Thank you," he said softly.

Kenna smiled and turned to face him. She was savoring every moment of Frang in her cottage. Tomorrow morning, she would be alone once more.

5

Frang stared at the ceiling above him. It had been a long and sleepless night. Knowing Kenna was only a few feet from him in her bed brought delicious visions of erotic enticement into his mind and body leaving little room for sleep. How he'd love to cover her body with his, licking and kissing her delectable breasts until she cried out for more. He'd cover her sex with his hand and find her hidden pearl, stroking it until she peaked. Then he'd take her, fill her with his rod, and thrust into her until she had drained him of his seed. He shifted to ease his aching cock and knew if he didn't turn his mind to other things, he'd take Kenna like he'd been dreaming of doing.

His hand rose and he gently touched the wound from the day before. It was nearly healed, and he knew it didn't have anything to do with Kenna's herbs. He had assumed that once the curse was over, he would no longer be immortal. It was something he definitely needed to speak to Aimery about post-haste.

The rustle of movement alerted him Kenna was waking. He silently rose and began the fire. Once the fire was roaring, he glanced at her to see her on her side with her back to him. Frang smiled as he straightened and imagined pulling the covers away from her inch by inch. He'd curve his body around hers and reach around to thumb her nipples until they were hard, aching peaks. He'd lift her top leg and slowly enter her, circling her swollen pearl. Since he couldn't do that, he walked from the house.

Outside, he took a deep breath and tried to get his raging body under control. He turned his thoughts to the Druids and wondered how they were doing at the Glen without him. After the laird's visit the day before, he fully expected Wallace to send someone to check on Kenna. Frang would have to be on his way soon. But not yet.

He moved to the small pile of wood stacked to be chopped. The battle yesterday left sore muscles this morning, but it was a good sore.

Frang let his hand curl around the handle of the axe as he grinned. Being the High Priest at the Glen had afforded him a certain position, one that didn't do this sort of menial labor. He wondered what the Druids would think of him now that he was anxious to do such labor. Over the last five years, tasks like this one had honed muscles ignored before and given him added strength.

With a slight yank, he pulled the axe from the stump and bent to pick up a rather large piece of wood. With one deep breath, Frang lifted the axe and drove it into the wood.

Kenna yawned and stretched before she remembered

she wasn't the only one in her cottage. She rose and glanced at the pallet Frang had made before the hearth, only to find him gone. Disappointment filled her as she swung her legs over the bed and rose.

She let out a breath as she walked to the roaring fire and put the kettle of water on to boil. It was then she heard the steady sound of chopping. She moved to her window and pushed open the shutters to find Frang chopping wood.

If she'd thought he looked good yesterday standing in her cottage or fighting the Carmichaels, it was nothing to how he looked this morning with his shirt off and his torso gleaming with sweat as his muscles bunched and flexed with each swing of the axe.

He was by far the most alluring and handsome man she had ever laid eyes upon. Too bad he wasn't hers to spend the day in bed with him teaching her all the ways a man could take a woman. She had never thought to want to mate with a man, but with Frang, that's all she could think about.

Suddenly, he stopped and turned to look at her. His chest rose and fell from his exertion. He gave her a smile before he turned back to the wood.

Kenna stepped back with a smile of her own, her middle clutching. There was something different about Frang. She couldn't lay her finger on it, but it was there.

Her mind wandered over what she had seen and learned from him as she set about making their morning meal. It wasn't until he walked into the cottage with his hair wet from a recent dunking in the rain barrel that she realized how his presence dominated.

Rarely did she share her meals with anyone. She had always hated being alone, but that was a healer's fate, one she had accepted long ago.

"You'll have firewood to last you awhile. You really should have someone come and help you around here."

"I rarely get coin in payment. Instead, I'll get chickens or pigs or an hour of a man's time to tend to the chopping or whatever else I need done."

Frang pushed strands of wet hair off his face. "Is there a lot you need done?"

"Isn't there always something to be done?" she asked with a laugh as she readied their meal.

It wasn't until they were nearly done with the meal that she felt his eyes on her. Kenna raised her gaze. "Say what is on your mind."

"Why don't I stay for a few days and see about fixing some of the things you need."

Kenna sat back and regarded him. Her first reaction was one of excitement that he didn't plan to leave. As much as she'd like to think he was doing this out of the kindness of his heart she had learned the hard way that people expected some kind of payment.

"What do you want in return?"

Frang winced at the hardness in her tone. He had hoped to broach the subject of him staying without causing her to think he had ulterior motives. He sighed and rested his arms on the table.

"Your company. And just that," he hurried to say before she could get a word in. "I'm in no hurry to continue to my destination. Also, I like it here. I like you. I want nothing more from you than conversation and a nice meal."

She regarded him warily. Suspiciously. Was he mistaken in the desire he had seen in her eyes yesterday? Did he want her so badly he was reading more into Kenna's touches than what they were—a healer using her abilities?

"I'm not helpless," she said. "I can take care of myself."

Frustration spiked through him. "Like you did with those three men ready to have their way with you?"

"I had a dagger in my basket," she said defensively.

"A weapon in your basket isn't worth much if the basket gets taken or knocked away. You need it somewhere on you at all times."

"Like where?"

"Strap it to your leg under your skirts where no one knows you have a weapon. It puts you at an advantage, which is what you need."

"A good suggestion. I'll do that."

"Do you know how to use the dagger?"

She laughed. "If you mean, could I kill a man with it? Aye, I can."

"Good. As I was saying, I am simply offering my services if you so desire them. If not, I will leave immediately."

Her gaze briefly lowered to the floor. When she spoke, her voice was low and soft. "Only for a few days."

Frang bowed his head slightly to hide the smile he couldn't keep hidden. He hadn't known until that moment just how much he wanted to stay with her, even if he never tasted her sweet lips. "As you wish."

He rose and walked to the door before he stopped. Without turning toward her he said, "Just say the word and I'll leave forever."

He didn't wait for her response as he opened the door and stepped outside. His feet took him to the wood he had chopped. The first order of business was stacking the wood. Then, he'd see about the pen that held the pig.

* * *

Aimery, his feet resting on his large table, looked out of his wide window at the city of *Caer Rhoemyr*, his thoughts on Frang.

He was so caught up in his thoughts he never heard Theron walk into the room until he stood beside the table. With a sigh, Aimery chuckled at his king's grin.

"Stop gloating. It doesn't become you," Aimery said.

Theron laughed as he leaned against the wall next to the window. "Why? I don't get to gloat often, especially not with you. So, old friend, tell me what has captured your thoughts so heavily that you didn't hear me enter the room?"

"Frang."

"Ah," Theron said, nodding. "He's been good for the Druids. I hate that he had to leave the Glen."

"He didn't have to."

Theron turned from the window, his royal cloak of white and silver billowing behind him. "He did. Give your friend some credit. All will work out as it should."

"Will it?" Aimery asked as he dropped his feet to the floor and stood. "Too many times we've come so close to losing it all. What if this time we do?"

"It is a chance we have to take. Frang must make this journey, Aimery. You know that."

Aimery nodded reluctantly. "You tell me nothing I don't already know."

"Then trust Frang to make the right choices. He is a good man."

Aimery turned his head to Theron. "A man who shouldn't have been tricked and then cursed. You could have told him what he needed to do and given him the immortality. For three hundred years he has thought he did something wrong."

Theron moved toward the door then stopped. "We could have, but we didn't. Not all humans respond as we'd like, so we learned to deal with them as we did Frang. It has always worked. Trust that it will this time, as well."

Aimery waited until his king left his office before he ran a hand down his face. He walked to the window and looked out over the royal kingdom. So often of late they had battled evil. He wanted peace, for himself and his friends on Earth.

* * *

Unable to hold off any longer, Kenna took a goblet of water outside to Frang. She had not consciously avoided him, but then she hadn't needed to with her work as well as her clansmen coming to her for their needs. And just as her laird had promised, a patrol had been by twice to check on her.

Now there was nothing keeping her from going to Frang. She smoothed back her unruly hair from her face and grabbed the goblet as she walked from the cottage.

Halfway to Frang she wished she had taken a moment to brush and replait her hair.

Then, silently chastised herself for wanting to look good for him. She was still shaking her head at herself when she turned the corner of her cottage and saw him finish righting the pen for the pig.

All thought left her as he looked over his shoulder at her and grinned a boyish, devilish grin that made her insides melt. If only she dared enough to let him know what she wanted.

Be careful, Kenna. He's leaving, and that means heartache for you.

"Ah, you must have read my mind," Frang said as he walked toward her, stopping near the corner of the cottage.

"Wh...what?" she stammered.

He motioned to the goblet. "My throat is parched. You must have read my mind."

Kenna forced a smiled. "Aye."

He gave her a wink just before he plunged his head in the barrel of rainwater. He straightened and flipped back his hair, sending water all over her.

Kenna couldn't stop the laughter that bubbled over. Her laughter only intensified when she looked at Frang to see his long, dark hair dripping over his face and shoulders and his mouth gaping at the frigid temperature of the water.

"Just what I needed," he said as he smoothed back his hair. "Come," he beckoned her.

She was holding out the goblet to him when he shook his head like a dog, spraying her even more. Her laughter started all over again as she tried to shield her face while not spilling the water.

By the time she finished laughing, she had to wipe her eyes. She pushed on her cheeks to try and stop them from hurting so, yet every time she looked at Frang, she wanted to laugh again.

He now leaned against the cottage drinking his water and eying her with a sly grin that said he had done everything a purpose.

"That felt good." Kenna moved to look at the pen, hoping Frang didn't realized how lonely her life was by that simple sentence.

He grunted in response. "Laughter sometimes is the best cure."

Kenna turned her head to look at him. "Cure for what?"

"Loneliness. Boredom. Anger. Any number of emotions."

She smiled, relieved he hadn't discovered her secret. "I agree. You did a good job on the pen. Thank you."

He shrugged. "My pleasure."

"It's nearing noon. I've fixed our meal."

He walked with her into the cottage. "You were busy this morn. Is it normally that way?"

"Not always. Some days are slower than others."

"Hmm. Is there anything in particular you'd like me to work on next?"

Kenna shrugged as she set his trencher in front of him. "You've worked hard all morning. Take the afternoon off."

"Is that what you're doing?"

Her gaze jerked to him as he sat. “In a way. I’m going to look for the herbs I wasn’t able to find yesterday.”

“Then I’ll come with you.”

She started to tell him she didn’t need him, but after recalling yesterday, she changed her mind. Besides, she told herself, she’d enjoy the company.

6

Frang leaned against a thick oak and watched Kenna walk around the forest. To the untrained eye, it would appear as if she wandered aimlessly. But Frang knew better.

Her steps were light, almost as if she floated on the ground, afraid to disturb even one fallen leaf.

She was amazing to watch. Even when her hand went deep into briars, it came away unscathed. It wasn't just her beauty that was flawless. It was her soul. Frang was struck speechless as the realization hit him.

Kenna was a Druid.

How he hadn't seen it immediately he didn't know, but it was laid bare before him now. It could be because she wasn't with other Druids, so she didn't know how to bring out her Druid abilities.

He blew out a deep breath. She needed to be in the Glen, but he doubted she would go on her own. And he couldn't return. Not now, not ever.

Needing to turn his thoughts, Frang pushed away from

the tree and walked to Kenna. "What do you search so diligently for?"

Her amber eyes glowed with surprise. "Linden. Have you heard of it?"

"Aye." As soon as he spoke, he realized he had inadvertently let her know he was much more than just a simple man. Yet, she didn't show any outward signs of surprise.

She smiled. "Good. You'll know what to look for. I've had to use much of it of late. I've had to search farther and farther from my cottage each time."

"That is a strange herb to use," he said cautiously. In fact, many used it to kill, but he knew if used with magic there were other outcomes.

"Not so strange," she said. "In the right doses it can kill, aye, but it can also cure fever and heal some wounds."

"I defer to your judgment as a healer." What she said was true, but Frang couldn't shake the feeling that someone, somewhere was using this herb for other means.

As a Druid and friend of the Fae he felt compelled to learn who and why. Then put a stop to it. In whatever manner he had to.

"Do you mind if I ask who is using the herb?"

Out of the corner of his eye he saw her pause and glance at him, but he kept his attention on the ground searching for the elusive plant.

"The bulk of the use is at the castle," she finally answered. "Why?"

He shrugged. "I'm curious by nature. Any time something is used more than others I find myself wondering why." He hoped she bought the lie. "Are many of the soldiers wounded then?"

"Nay. Laird Wallace likes to give his men a little of the herb every month. To keep them healthy." The last part she said in a deep voice mimicking Wallace himself.

Frang looked up and smiled at her. "As a healer, I would have thought you'd find his words nonsense."

"Though I learned everything I know from Brigit, she died before I could fully complete my training. Before I did any healing, I had to learn every herb and its main uses to memory. So, while I may not know every use for an herb, I know which can kill a man."

Frang regarded her silently, wondering how much he could tell her. If he could trust her. "Some say that there is magic in some herbs."

"An old wives' tale."

Though she said it in jest, he saw the wariness in her gaze. She was hiding something. And she didn't trust him. Not that he blamed her. She didn't know him. He'd have to remedy that. His first thought was to pull her against him and claim her lips in a kiss that left her breathless and her body craving him as much as he yearned for her. His hunger for her had grown into something he was having a difficult time controlling.

And the fact was, he didn't want to control it. He wanted to release his desire for her and let it consume them both.

Frang shook his head to clear it and focused. He couldn't kiss her to gain her trust, though it was an alternative he wished he could take. Nay, he'd have to prove he was trustworthy first.

"I found some," he called out as he spotted the linden. He knelt and began to pick the delicate flowers as Kenna rushed to his side.

She squatted beside him and held out her basket for him to put the flowers in. "Don't take them all," she cautioned.

After he had picked half the flowers, they rose and began walking through the forest once more.

"How much more do you need?" He eyed her full basket.

She shrugged. "As much as I can find. I don't like having to come out here every day, and since I wasn't able to find any yesterday, I need to make up several days' worth."

"Does Wallace have so many men then?"

She cast him an anxious glance. "He likes to keep them stocked."

"They won't do anyone any good if they're wilted." He knew he pushed her, but he had to know the truth.

She stopped and turned to face him, her amber eyes hard and accusing. "Are you saying I'm a liar?"

"Nay. I'm asking you to tell me what the linden is really for."

She gave a bark of laughter. "I did."

"Then either you've lied about knowing herbs or you've lied about what the Wallace wants them for."

Her eyes grew round with indignation. "How dare you."

Frang closed his eyes and sighed. When he opened them, Kenna had walked away. He hurried to catch up with her. He reached out and grasped her arm, but she yanked it away from him and quickened her steps.

"Kenna. Stop and let me explain." But she wasn't listening.

He lengthened his strides and took her arm again. This time when she jerked her arm away, she sent her basket flying and the herbs spilling onto the ground.

"Nay," she cried as she looked to the herbs.

But Frang wasn't about to pay attention to anything but her. He pushed her against a tree. The words he had been about to say were lost as he gazed into her amber eyes. Her breasts were pressed against his chest, and he felt every one of her soft curves, making his body explode with desire. His rod throbbed with need.

Frang's eyes lowered to her lips that he had dreamed of kissing, lips that were just breathes from him. He found his head lowering to hers as everything faded away but her.

A falcon screamed overhead, breaking the spell Frang had been under. He lifted his head and took a steadying breath before he tried to speak.

"I have my reasons for asking those questions. I know you don't trust me, and I don't blame you, but the fact is, I know herbs. From what you've told me, the Wallace is using them for other than what he's said."

Her eyes narrowed and her nostrils flared as rage ran through her. "I'm surprised you haven't accused me of being an accomplice."

"Are you?"

"Get your hands off of me," she screeched as she struggled against him.

Frang held her with both arms, then had to use his body to keep her from kicking him in the groin. Her fighting him only reminded him how desperately he needed a female.

His body responded to hers instantly. She must have felt his rod pressed into her stomach for she quit moving and glared at him.

"What do you want?"

He released her and backed away. "I told you. I want to know the real reason you're bringing linden to your laird."

She didn't answer him as she fell to her knees and began to gently pick up the scattered herbs.

"Kenna."

She shook her head. "Don't. I thought you were someone different, someone who wasn't trying to steal my supposed secrets or accuse me of being a witch."

Frang stilled. "Someone has tried to steal your secrets?"

An impatient breath left her lips as she rose to her feet, basket in hand. "I don't have any secrets. Healing isn't for everyone, it's a gift. Yet, some would think otherwise. Someone went through my cottage a fortnight ago and ransacked my entire backroom. I've been trying to fill the herbs I've lost."

"Jesu," Frang exclaimed as he raked a hand through his hair. He met her gaze. "And the witch part?"

She visibly shivered, telling him it bothered her even now to talk about it. "About a month back someone grabbed me from behind as I was walking to my cottage. He asked me about specific herbs and their uses, then told me he knew I used magic and he'd see me burned as a witch."

Frang began to pace as his mind worked over her words. "You didn't see the man?"

"Nay. It was at night, and I was so scared that as soon as he released me, I ran inside the cottage."

"The right thing to do," he said.

Kenna watched as Frang paced in front of her. His sky-blue eyes held more worry than she had ever seen. She still wasn't sure why she had told him of the incidents. She hadn't even gone to her laird about it. For one, because she knew Wallace would insist, she move within the castle walls, and she refused to leave her cottage. And two, because she liked the forest surrounding her.

"What herbs did the man ask you about?"

She hesitated. She had hoped he wouldn't ask. "Linden and Wolf's Bane."

He stopped and stared at her. "Poisons."

"Aye."

"Do you often have them in your collection?"

"I do. Though they are poisons, they can also be used to heal in very small doses."

He ran a hand down his face as he sighed. "I have an inkling that the attack yesterday wasn't by chance."

"I had the same thought."

His blue eyes narrowed on her. "You weren't going to tell me any of this, were you?"

"Why should I? You are a stranger passing through. This isn't your problem."

"It is now. I would not be the man I am if I left without ensuring you are safe."

She snorted and turned back to the cottage. "Frang, there are dangers around every corner. You cannot protect me from everything."

"True, but I can protect you from whoever is trying to hurt you now."

They walked silently back to the cottage. She wondered how long he would wait before he again asked her about the linden and its use at the castle.

She had a decision to make. Tell him the truth. Or lie again.

7

Nearly a week had passed since the confrontation in the forest, but it was all Kenna had thought about. Frang had not asked her again about the herbs, though she knew he wanted to. Instead, he spent his days fixing the various and assorted problems in and around her cottage.

She still hadn't determined whether to tell him the truth or lie once again about the herbs and their use. It made it even more difficult to decide since she couldn't get the image of him pressed against her out of her mind.

No man had ever been that close to her. No man had ever looked at her the way she sometimes caught him staring at her, as if he were starving and she was his meal. She knew it was his rod that she had felt against her. Just thinking he might want her sent her blood pounding and her heart racing. In all her years of wanting a husband, she had never thought about what it would feel like to have someone want her body.

The more she thought about it, the more she found it difficult to concentrate on anything else.

She tied together a string of sage to hang to dry as she found herself wondering what it would be like to kiss Frang. Every night as he lay near her, she thought of him. Each day that he stayed with her, she found herself growing more attached to him.

A chilling thought for someone who was always alone.

A thought that should have kept her mindful of her future. Yet, one look into his beautiful sky-blue eyes and she was lost. Lost as a leaf on the wind.

How she wished Brigit was still around to talk to. The old healer would have known what to say, which direction to lead her. Now, Kenna was left floundering on her own.

"Kenna?"

Her head jerked up to find Frang at the entrance to her backroom. "Something wrong?"

"I was about to ask you the same thing," he said as he leaned casually against the doorway. "You look troubled."

She shrugged and reached above her to hang the herbs. Her gaze quickly returned to Frang to find him watching her. "Tell me something of your past," she begged.

"What would you like to know?"

"Something few people know."

"Like what? What my childhood was like? What I really thought of my parents?"

She shook her head and slowly came around the table until she was only a few steps from him. "Something secret."

His eyes searched hers. One heartbeat. Two. Three. "I've seen Druids."

She couldn't have been more shocked if he said he was king. "Truly?"

His lips turned up in a smile. "Aye. 'Tis true. Druids still exist and practice in Scotland."

"If they are caught, they'll be burned."

"They won't be caught."

He sounded so sure of himself that she wanted to believe, needed to believe. If there were other Druids, maybe she could search them out and finish the training Brigit had begun.

"Where?" she suddenly asked. The desperation to know their whereabouts was strong, overriding everything else.

"You want to know their location?"

She nodded, trying to keep her excitement minimal.

"Why?" He pushed off the doorway and took a step toward her. "So, you can find them and release their location to others who can kill them?"

"Nay," Kenna tried to say but his words drowned hers.

He took another step bringing his body within breaths of hers. "Why, Kenna? Give me one good reason why I should put them in danger?"

She looked into his eyes and wanted desperately to tell him the truth. Instead, she told him half of it. "I've heard of Druids from Brigit. She spoke highly of them. I didn't think there were any more in Scotland."

He tilted toward her causing her to lean back over the table. His lips hovered over hers and his eyes darkened. For the briefest of moments, she thought he might kiss her.

"Nay," he said softly. "If you want to see them, I will take you to them, but I won't give you, their location."

She blinked. "You'll take me."

He nodded and straightened. But his gaze never left hers. "Do you want to go?"

Of course, she wanted to go, but that meant she'd have to leave her clan, the only place she had ever known. She wasn't the adventurous sort.

* * *

Frang saw the exhilaration die in her eyes. When she had asked for a secret, for a moment he had contemplated telling her his biggest one of all.

"I cannot leave my clan." Her voice was low and held a note of sorrow. She turned her back to him.

Frang raked his gaze over her slender form. He could still feel her warm breath on his neck as he leaned over her, still see the wanting in her amber eyes as her lips parted slightly. It would have been so easy to bend his head and capture her plump lips with his own.

"Think on it," he said.

He left the cottage and walked into the forest. There wasn't much left for him to repair, which left him no reason to stay. Yet, he knew he had to. It was his Druid sense that told him to stay, to stay until Kenna was out of danger.

There was no doubt in his mind she was in imminent danger. He just wished he knew who it was from.

Since their argument while gathering herbs, Frang had not broached the subject again, hoping she would learn to trust him. But trust wasn't an easy thing to learn. When she had asked for a secret, he'd known it was the perfect opportunity for him to show her he was a man to be trusted.

He would do what he had to do to earn her trust, all the

while praying he managed to keep her alive in the meantime.

The sound of laughter made him turn toward the cottage. He spotted her leaning out the window of her workroom as she laughed at the antics of two birds. As soon as the birds flew off, she tilted her head to the side and got a faraway look in her eyes.

She was dreaming of something, and he couldn't help but wonder if it was him. Did she feel the same need as he? Did she not sense the desire between them, discern the heady passion?

Frang groaned and turned away from her. He had to find some release. It had been too long since he had found a woman. Maybe his need was leading him to believe there was something between him and Kenna when there really wasn't.

And the only way to discover that was for him to find another woman.

Immediately.

He spun back around to the cottage and called out for Kenna. She met him at the door, her gaze guarded and worried. "You told me today was market day, aye?"

She nodded.

"I'm going to market." Her face dropped and he realized she thought he was leaving. He was almost angry enough to let her believe that. "Is there anything you need?"

A relieved smiled pulled at her lips. "Nay. When will you return?"

Her last words had come out quickly, breathlessly. As if

she feared being alone again. He understood that fear all too well.

"Maybe tonight. Most likely tomorrow."

"I see."

"Nay, you don't," he corrected her. "You'll know when I leave, lass. Ken?"

She smiled though it didn't reach her eyes. "I ken. Be safe. Wallace's soldiers can be belligerent at times."

"'Tis they that should worry about me." He bent and grasped his sword he had leant against the cottage in case of emergencies. He pushed his arm through the strap then pulled the leather over his head until the sword rested in the valley of his back.

"You have the dagger?" he asked.

She touched her leg. "'Tis strapped to my thigh, just as you told me. It's within easy reach."

Nothing had happened while he had been with her, but the steady stream of her clansmen seeking cures for their ailments left little time for anyone to bother her.

With a small nod, he turned on his heel and started for the road that would lead him to the castle.

* * *

Kenna watched Frang walk away with a sense of dread. He had told her he would return, but she hadn't been able to discern if he was lying or not. When he had first stated he was headed to the castle, she had thought he was leaving. For good. And the panic that set in caused her to think about Frang and what he had come to mean to her in a very short time. It almost wasn't fair that she had come to crave his gaze on her, to hear his deep voice as he spoke to her or that she loved his company during mealtimes.

Slowly, Kenna turned and entered the cottage. She shut the door behind her and leaned against it. She would be alone again. Suddenly, her cottage was silent and empty, as if all the life had left with Frang.

How easily she had come to accept Frang in her little world. How readily she had welcomed his presence as if he had always belonged there. It let her know just how lonely she had become. So lonely in fact, that she'd welcomed a stranger into her home when she hadn't allowed any of her clansmen.

If she moved to the castle as the Wallace wanted, at least she wouldn't be alone as she was now. At least she would have people around her at all times.

You don't have to be alone to be lonely, Kenna.

She cursed her conscious. A healer she wanted to be, but she never intended to grow old with no husband or children by her side. Besides, after the two attacks and someone rummaging through her herbs, her laird would see her safe inside the castle walls eventually. She could only hold him off for so long.

8

Frang stepped through the gates of Wallace castle and let his gaze wander. It wasn't a large castle, but it was well defended. Guards stood atop the battlements, their eyes searching the horizon for an enemy. More guards stood in the gatehouse, and two more stood on either side of the gate.

The castle itself consisted of a rectangular fortress enclosed by two lines of walls that formed the inner and outer bailey. The inner bailey housed a tower at each corner and a large gatehouse in the middle of the west front.

His gaze shifted as he looked for the postern door, he knew was somewhere near leading to the outer bailey. He found it to his left as he spotted two women walking through it. It was valuable knowledge if he needed to leave in a hurry.

As he slowly made his way toward the postern door, Frang noted the chapel near the southeast tower. The well stood just to the right of the chapel with the entrance to the castle on the left of the chapel.

With it being market day, vendors lined the bailey hawking their wares as men and women bargained for their needs. It would be a great day to do some looking around the castle without being noticed.

But he wasn't there for that.

A woman walked into his line of vision and gave him an appreciative onceover before she winked. Now that, that was what he'd come for. Despite the fact he wanted Kenna with a ferocity that frightened him, he could relieve his ache with another woman.

Frang smiled and went to follow the women when he saw a group of guards walk through the postern door. He glanced at the woman to find her waiting for him. His instinct prodded him to discover more about the laird and his need for Kenna's herbs, and despite his wish to relieve his aching rod, the information was more valuable. With a growl of frustration, Frang followed the soldiers.

When he stepped into the outer bailey, he was amazed at the amount of people who lived within the castle walls. Wallace may not have a large castle, but he kept his people safe.

No one stopped Frang as he wandered aimlessly taking in all aspects of the outer bailey before he once more returned to the inner bailey. His gaze went to the castle as he again wondered why Wallace needed so much linden from Kenna.

If Kenna wouldn't tell him, maybe the guards would. He walked to the group he had seen earlier. It didn't take them long to notice him.

"Halt," one burly Highlander called.

Frang stopped and smiled. "Good afternoon, lads. I was passing through and thought I would stop and see the great Wallace castle."

Just as he suspected, his words made the men puff up. "Aye," the burly man stated. "We are the Wallace clan. Who are ye?"

"Frang Malcolm," he said with a sweeping bow.

"Yer a long way from Malcolm lands."

Frang straightened and let his gaze touch each of the soldiers. "I'm sowing some wild oats." He grinned and waited.

He didn't have long to wait. The burly man laughed and stepped aside. "I remember sowing some wild oats meself," he said as he handed Frang a mug of ale.

"Ye still are sowing 'em, Rory."

Rory chuckled and raised his mug before he tilted it to his lips.

Frang settled against the wall beside Rory and took a long drink of the ale. Getting next to them had been easy. Convincing them to tell him castle secrets was another.

But he wasn't a Druid High Priest for nothing.

* * *

Kenna told herself she wasn't going to the castle to spy on Frang, she was going to deliver the herbs her laird needed. If she happened to see Frang while she was there, so be it. If not, she certainly wouldn't search him out.

The sun was sinking fast in the sky when she reached the huge gates of Wallace castle.

"'Tis late, Kenna," one of the guards said.

She nodded hello to the guard. "Aye. I came as soon as I could."

Without waiting for the guard to comment, she walked through the gate and into the bailey. The castle stood before her like a stone giant. Inside, a powerful laird waited for her.

Her hands shook as she continued toward the castle, looking neither left nor right as many of the vendors headed home. Her steps didn't falter as she climbed the steep steps to the castle door. It wasn't until she reached for the door that her legs began to quake. Before she could push on the door, it was yanked open.

And she found herself staring at the Wallace.

"Kenna," he said with a bright smile. His golden hair was pulled away from his face and held at the nape of his neck by a strip of leather. "You've come late."

She stepped inside the castle. "Aye. I knew you wanted the herbs as soon as I could find them."

His dark eyes raked over her. "You're just in time for the evening meal. Come. Sit by me," he said as he took the basket from her and handed it to a guard near the door.

Kenna let him lead her to the dais at the back of the great hall. Her gaze roamed over the hall noting the many guards standing against the walls.

"That is new," she commented, nodding to the large tapestry hanging behind the dais. It showed a great battle scene with a man being crowned in the middle.

"Aye. James' wife finished it just a few days ago. Do you like it?"

She nodded as she looked over the work. She knew

James and his wife well since they had been trying unsuccessfully to get with child. "Very much."

He beamed. "I'll be sure to let James' wife know. She's very fond of you."

Kenna grew uneasy at his words. Why would he care what she thought of the tapestry? She hesitated when she saw he planned to sit her on his left, a place that was saved for a wife.

"Something amiss?"

She looked into his dark eyes. He had a face of an angel, but she feared his heart was that of the devil. "Nay," she finally answered. "I'm just surprised I've been given such a high honor."

He waited until she sat before, he lowered himself into his chair and turned to her. "You are our healer, Kenna. You are prized among the people. I only show you the respect you deserve."

"Thank you." Her voice shook and she hoped he took it to mean she was flattered not frightened out of her wits. She swallowed and gripped her hands together under the table. "I hope I haven't interfered with anything."

His brows furrowed. "I beg your pardon?"

"You were leaving the castle when you found me."

"Ah." He chuckled and tucked a strand of hair behind her ear. "It is nothing that cannot wait. I'm so very pleased that you are here."

She lowered her gaze, unable to hold his. She was saved from having to say anything by the arrival of the food. Thankfully, most of her laird's attention was taken by his first in command seated on his other side.

Yet, Kenna enjoyed her meal. It was the first time in

quite awhile that she hadn't fixed her own meal. Her gaze roamed leisurely around the great hall taking in the laughter and merriment of the occupants, giving her entertainment as she ate.

"You look amused."

Wallace's voice close to her ear made her start. She shrugged. "I enjoy watching people."

Out of the corner of her eye, she watched as he looked out over the great hall. "It must be hard to live alone."

"Sometimes," she admitted.

He turned fully toward her. "You should have more meals here at the castle with me."

Kenna laughed, flattered. "I do not like returning home so late."

"Another reason to live within my walls, Kenna. Then I could see you whenever I wanted."

There were times Kenna knew she could be a little naïve, but this wasn't one of them. It was obvious by the way Wallace stared at her that he wanted much more than her company at mealtimes.

She cleared her throat. "I heard a rumor a couple of months back that you had found a bride."

He shook his head, the smile never leaving his face. "Nay. I've not taken a bride."

This time Kenna smiled. "Not taking a bride is vastly different than finding one."

"Oh, I found one. She just hasn't agreed yet." His voice was smooth, seductive.

Kenna shifted in her seat. "I hope she agrees soon, my laird. 'Tis been awhile since the castle has had a mistress."

"Never fear, my sweet. I plan to give the Wallace clan a new mistress verra soon."

With her mind reeling, Kenna turned her head... and spotted Frang amid some of the soldiers. And with a woman on each leg. Her stomach knotted and her heart plummeted to her feet as she stared at his profile. Vaguely, she realized what she felt was jealousy, jealousy over a man she barely knew and didn't trust.

But he had been hers for a precious week. Hers. Her own.

She hurriedly turned her head away before Frang noticed her gaze. Dimly, she heard Wallace talking, but she was trying desperately to get the image of Frang with two women out of her mind.

"Kenna?"

She jerked her head to her laird. "Did you say something?"

"Aye. Since it is so late, I asked if you'd like to stay the night."

She nodded, her mind already back on Frang and his easy conquest of the women. Were they the first two he'd had? Or had he already had a few women? He'd said he was coming to the castle for market, but he must have come for other reasons. She felt so stupid to have thought he wanted her, for if he had, he would have tried to kiss her.

When Wallace extended his hand to her, Kenna took it without thought and let him pull her from the table. She followed him to the chairs before the hearth. All the while he talked, but she never heard a word.

She refused to look to where she had last seen Frang. Indeed, she kept her eyes trained on the roaring fire as its orange and blue flames leapt skyward as if they would break way. Kenna understood their need much more than she wanted. For she understood what the flames did not. She was trapped.

A touch on her arm brought her out of her thoughts. She looked up to find Wallace holding her hand, a small smile on his lips.

She let her gaze wonder over his face with his square jaw, a roguish chin with a dimple in the middle. His nose held a bit of patrician in its long, lean lines. His dark eyes were wide set and regarded her with intensity.

"Everyone is retiring for the night."

"Oh." She jumped to her feet and turned toward the hall. Her gaze unwittingly went to the spot she had last seen Frang. He was no longer there. He was no longer even in the great hall she noted as she let her gaze sweep over the people.

Just as well, she thought as she started to look for a place to sleep for the night.

"Where are you going, Kenna?"

She glanced over her shoulder. "To find a place to sleep, of course."

In the next instant, he had captured her hand again. His need to touch her unsettled her, but she kept her expression bland as she turned to him.

"You aren't sleeping down here. I've had a chamber prepared for you."

Her mouth opened, but he put a finger to her lips. "Shh..." he whispered. "Let me take care of you."

Kenna stood stock still as his finger traced the line of

her lips. There was no denying it now. He wanted her. She trembled and saw Wallace smile.

"Aye, you feel it to, don't you? In a few months we can make it known that you'll be my new bride. No one will be surprised."

No one but me.

Kenna didn't object when he led her up the stairs to her chamber. With her heart drumming in her chest, she prayed he wouldn't try to kiss her. When they reached the chamber, he opened the door and brought her inside.

"Do you approve?"

Kenna glanced around the room noting the dark green bed hangings, the chest at the foot of the bed, small pegs in the wall and the table and chair by the hearth.

"'Tis very nice. Thank you."

"Only the best for you," he said.

Her breath lodged in her throat as he walked to her. She nearly let out a loud sigh when he grasped her hand and brought it to his lips. "Until the morn, my sweet."

Kenna counted to twenty after he left before she walked to the door and bolted it. She leaned against the wood and covered her face with her hands.

Most women would be overjoyed to find their laird had picked them for his bride. But not Kenna. As she explored her feelings against Wallace, she knew part of it was because of his need for the linden, but that could be forgiven.

What was it, then, that kept her from embracing the future he offered her? She would no longer be alone. She'd have an entire clan to look after, much as she already did, but in a different manner. She'd have a husband with whom she could grow old, and hopefully children to fill her days with laughter.

But deep in her heart, she knew she'd be better off alone than as the Wallace's bride.

She pushed off the door and slowly walked to the bed. Her mind wandered to Frang. It had felt like a knife in her chest to see him with those women, and for the rest of meal she alternated between wanting him to see her and hoping he didn't. Her hand grazed the dark green coverlet. Suddenly, she was weary to the bone. She crawled onto the bed and let her eyes drift shut.

With all her might she wished herself to sleep, to drift in the darkness unaware and unfeeling. Even if only for a brief time.

9

Frang gently pulled his arm from underneath the woman's head and crawled over another until he stood by the door. He cursed himself for ten kinds of fool for not taking his pleasure with one, or both, of the women. He had told himself he needed information, but the simple truth was all he could think of was Kenna. It had been easy to get them drunk, and all the while he had played the sotted fool.

But acting drunk had revealed several secrets.

With one last look at the sleeping women, he walked from the small cottage. His gaze scanned the outer bailey, but the only movement he saw was the guards walking the battlements.

Using the shadows, he crept slowly and silently to the postern door that led to the inner bailey. The guards he had drunk with at the evening meal were slumped against the wall, their snores loudly filling the air.

Frang chuckled to himself and kept to the shadows as

he moved into the bailey. Just like a ghost he crept around the castle until he came to the kitchen entrance.

Carefully, gradually, he opened the door and hurriedly stepped inside. The kitchen was thankfully deserted. He grabbed a loaf of bread and tore off a piece as he walked to the entrance into the great hall. As he stuffed a piece of bread into his mouth, he wondered if Kenna was safe and alone in her cottage. Many times, he'd felt eyes on him during the meal, but every time he had tried to turn to have a look at the laird and to see who was watching him, the women repeatedly distracted him.

How he wished he knew of another way to get to the Wallace's secret chamber he had learned about. There was, without a doubt, another way, but Frang didn't have the time to wander the castle. He needed his proof before he confronted Kenna in the morn.

At the kitchen doorway, he stood and surveyed the great hall. Bodies were everywhere. Some slept on the floor while others used the benches. In the corners, grouped together or alone, it didn't matter. He picked his way cautiously through the bodies. Mid-way across the great hall he spotted a couple kissing, the woman's skirts bunched at her waist and her arse bared as she rose and lowered herself on the man's rod.

It was all Frang could do not to groan aloud as he imagined the couple was him and Kenna. He could return to Kenna and take his pleasure except for the need to uncover the truth. Damn his righteousness.

He tamped down his desire for Kenna and continued through the great hall until he came to the stairs. Once again, he kept to the shadows and made his way up to the third floor. He looked down one corridor then the next to make sure no one was coming. As soon as he saw it was safe, he turned left and hurried to the stairs at the end of the hallway.

At the base of the stairs he listened, trying to discern if there was anyone was in the tower. After a moment, he crept up the stairs, his hand on the dagger on his hip in case he encountered anyone.

When he found the door, he stopped. The wooden door stood slightly ajar. Frang unsheathed his dagger and pushed the door open with his toe. His gaze scanned the tower, but seeing no one, he stepped inside.

He walked slowly around the tower taking in all he saw. It was much worse than he'd imagined. Much, much worse. The question was, was Kenna involved in it or was she an unwilling accomplice?

His finger reached out and touched the linden still in Kenna's basket.

Kenna's basket?

His stomach constricted painfully. She was here, or had been. The implication that she had waited until he left to come to the castle did not bode well for her innocence. And why would she come when she knew he was going to be here?

Granted, he had spent little time in the castle except for the meal, and then he had made sure the women were on his lap and his back to the dais so the Wallace wouldn't take notice of him.

Still, it rankled him that she had deceived him.

He turned to leave when his gaze landed on a large black tome. His breath left his body in a rush as he rushed toward the book, stumbling over a stool in the process. He stretched out a hand to touch the book and saw his hand shaking.

Frang opened his mouth to call to Aimery then realized he couldn't. He was no longer immortal. His call would most likely go unheard. He was on his own now.

He focused back on the tome. "Unbelievable," he murmured as he stroked a finger over the black leather.

The book was three hands' high, two wide, and at least a half a hand thick. All around the edges was the intricate knot work of the Fae, and in the middle of the tome was a large black stone with a blood red center.

"The Book of Magic," he whispered into the silent tower.

There was no doubt in his mind what the Wallace was doing now. He looked out the window and saw the black sky giving way to grey.

He had to get to Kenna and get some answers before he decided what to do about the book.

Kenna woke sometime before dawn unable to find the blessed darkness again. She looked over to the floor wishing she saw Frang sleeping there, but the stones were devoid of anything, even warmth.

She turned onto her back and looked at the top of the bed. When had her life become so...empty? Had it always been so, and just become more apparent lately because Frang had been with her?

There were no answers, though she didn't expect any.

She sat up and plucked at her skirts. She wished she had confided in Frang when she'd had the chance. Now she would have to deal with the Wallace on her own.

She feared he wouldn't take no for an answer. Yet, she had little choice. Before she changed her mind, she jumped from the bed and ran from the chamber. Her shoes pounded on the stone, but she didn't slow. She couldn't. She'd lose her nerve if she did.

When she came to the tower, she stopped at the stairs, her hand to her throat. She closed her eyes and took a deep breath before she started up the stairs. When she reached the top, she stood in shock at the open door.

Hesitantly, she peered inside but didn't find the Wallace or anyone else. She stepped into the tower and spotted her basket near the window. Her feet rushed forward as she grabbed the basket and turned to leave.

But that's when she saw the huge tome.

Kenna slowly turned around and looked at the book. Brigit had spoken of a tome that looked very much like the one she stared at. Unable to stop herself, she lifted the cover and gazed at the words in neat, bold lines that read The Book of Magic.

Surprise turned her blood to ice. The book was supposed to be a myth, but if her laird had it, it could only mean dangerous things for her and the rest of the clan. She quickly snatched up the heavy book and ran from the tower, stumbling in her haste and nearly falling down the curving stairs.

Kenna righted herself with a hand on the wall. She shifted the book in her arms and looped her arm through the basket handle. Using slow, measured steps she walked down the stairs. Every instinct in her told her to run as fast as she could, but she couldn't draw attention to herself. Not if she wanted to live.

How she made it out of the castle and into the stables without being stopped, she never knew. Nor did she encounter the Wallace. It was luck she hadn't expected.

The stable lad looked up as she entered. "The laird bade me fetch ye a horse if ye've a mind to have one to return to yer cottage."

Kenna blinked. "What?"

"Laird Wallace. He came to us last eve and told us to make sure we gave ye anything ye need. He said he expected you might wish to return to your cottage this morn, and he didn't want ye walkin'."

She almost laughed. Almost. Instead, she nodded to the lad. "A horse is what I require. A fast one."

* * *

Frang sprinted the last bit of distance to Kenna's cottage. As soon as he broke the clearing, he stopped and bent over with his hands on his knees as he gulped in air. No movement showed in the cottage, but then again, she should still be sleeping. He made himself walk to the cottage and open the door as if he didn't have a care in the world.

It wasn't until he looked to the bed, the empty bed, that real panic set in.

"Kenna," he said and rushed back outside as he looked to the castle.

10

Kenna had no idea where she was going. There wasn't time for her to return to her cottage. She sat atop her horse in the forest and closed her eyes, letting herself delve into her powers.

Which way?

No answer.

Please. I need to find the Druids. Which way?

East.

Her eyes flew open. Laughter bubbled up in her. She had heard it, her powers. Clear and distinct. Though her very life was in danger, a smile pulled at her lips as she turned the mare to the east and urged her into a gallop.

She was halfway out of the forest when she realized how close to her cottage she was. Since she had no food or a cloak, she needed to grab as much as she could. Besides, she wanted one last look at the cottage that had been the only home she had ever known.

As Kenna rode closer, her eyes misted with unshed

tears. She couldn't believe she was leaving. But she really didn't have a choice.

She stopped her horse and slid off its back, careful not to spill the basket. The reins dropped from her fingers as she slowly moved toward the cottage. It looked sad, as if it knew she was leaving for good. Kenna pushed open the door and stepped into her home. Her gaze looked over her belongings since she half expected the Wallace to be here waiting on her.

When she realized the cottage was as empty as it should be, she put the basket on the table and rushed to the backroom. She quickly grabbed a satchel and stuffed a few herbs into the bag. Then, she ran to the kitchen and wrapped a loaf of bread, some oatcakes, and a small block of cheese in a cloth and also stuffed it into the satchel.

She then spied the basket on the table. Her hand shook as she reached for the black tome. She lifted it and put it into the satchel behind the food and herbs. The fit was tight as the book was long and thick. She lifted the strap and walked to the door.

Just before she stepped outside, she gave one last glance over her home. Her gaze came to rest on the spot before the hearth where Frang had slept. She felt a pang in her heart at not being able to tell him goodbye, but maybe it was for the best. He'd ask questions. And she didn't have the answers he wanted.

With a deep breath, she walked from the cottage and to the waiting mare. She looped the satchel over her head and under one arm, so the strap ran diagonally across her body and the bag itself rested on her hip.

She mounted the mare and turned toward the east. A

click started the mare into a quick gallop that took her farther and farther away from her cottage to a new adventure, a new life.

One she was most excited to discover.

* * *

Frang raced through the forest, his blood pumping loudly in his ears. He kept telling himself to stay calm, that he'd find Kenna. Find her and make her explain everything to him.

He was so intent on thinking of Kenna that for a moment he thought it was his imagination that conjured her up atop a horse galloping through the forest. He stopped running and followed the horse with his eyes as it darted around trees and leapt over fallen logs.

"Kenna," he whispered when he spotted her flame red hair trailing behind her.

Immediately, Frang's gaze swung toward the castle. He expected to see the Wallace and his soldiers right behind Kenna, but only the sounds of the forest filled the air.

His eyes moved to where he'd last seen her and knew he had little choice. He turned and ran after her, praying he caught her before she did anything rash.

By the time he returned to the cottage, his side ached and sweat soaked his body. He pushed through the door, but Kenna was nowhere to be found.

"Kenna," he shouted as he walked to her backroom.

He took in the few herbs that littered the ground and had been trampled by hurried feet.

"Jesu, Kenna."

Frang turned and spotted the basket he had seen sitting in the Wallace's tower. The basket full of linden. Nothing made sense, least of all Kenna's odd behavior.

Just what was going on?

"Maybe you should ask her."

Frang swung around to find Aimery leaning against the doorway to Kenna's backroom. "Shite, Aimery. You scared ten years off my life."

Aimery chuckled and pushed away from the doorway. "You look...awful."

"And it is so nice to see you, too, old friend." Frang wasn't fooled. Aimery's presence meant something was off. "I hadn't expected to ever see you again."

Aimery's flaxen brow rose. "Did you take my friendship so lightly then?"

"Nay. I just assumed that since I am no longer cursed you would turn your attention to other things."

Aimery let out a breath and moved to the table. He leaned against the table, his hands on either side of Kenna's basket. "I never abandon friends, Frang. Never. You should have called to me."

"I thought about it." Frang watched the Fae commander carefully. Aimery's investigation of Kenna's herbs was telling.

Aimery looked up, his swirling blue eyes pinning him. "Do you know what these are?"

"Aye."

"You need to find her."

Frang ran a hand down his face. "That's what I'm trying to do."

Aimery closed his eyes and tilted his head back as if he

were listening to something. He opened his eyes and straightened. "She's headed East."

Frang stood rooted to the spot. East? To the Druid's Glen? Impossible. He had never told her where they were.

"What are you waiting for?" Aimery asked sharply.

Frang met his gaze. "There's something else. I found the Book of Magic."

"What?" Aimery's voice was so low and held such anger that he almost didn't hear him.

Frang nodded. "In a tower at Wallace castle."

"How did the Wallace get it?"

"That I don't know. I just happened across it."

Aimery turned and paced the small cottage. "If he has the book then there is no telling what he is trying to do."

"I know." Frang pointed to the basket when Aimery stopped and looked at him. "Those herbs, taken just the right way with just the right magic will make him immortal."

"Sons of the dragons," Aimery cursed. "I cannot touch the book for the magic was put into that book to battle the Fae. One touch would kill me."

Frang nodded. "I know."

"Why didn't you take it?"

"I thought I had more time. I just wanted to look around, to see if the Wallace was doing what I suspected. I thought he might be experimenting with trying to gain immortality with the linden herbs, but never once did it enter my mind he had found the Book of Magic."

"You should have taken it."

Frang nodded. "I know, but I didn't. I'll have to go back for it tonight."

Just then, the sound of approaching horses drew his attention. He went to step out of the cottage, but Aimery grabbed his arm.

"No need," the Fae said a moment before he made them invisible.

Frang stood silently as the front door was slammed open and the Wallace stepped into the cottage.

"Kenna," he bellowed. He looked strained, as if he had lost a prized jewel.

"Laird, a horse came through here," a soldier called from outside.

Wallace ran a hand down Kenna's bed. "She must have been taken," he said to himself. Then he raised his voice for his men. "Find her."

He was turning to go when Frang saw him spot the basket.

"Nay," the Wallace said in a pained whispered. "Kenna, nay. Not you."

Frang watched as the laird's face mottled with rage and he swiped the basket from the table before he stomped back to his men.

"The healer has taken a costly possession of mine. We'll return to the castle to get reinforcements then set out after her."

As soon as they were mounted and gone, Aimery lifted his hand from Frang, and the invisibility shield evaporated.

"It appears as if I don't need to return to the castle after all," Frang said as he turned to his friend.

Aimery regarded him silently. "Frang," he began.

"Don't," Frang stopped him. "I know what you would

say, and I would rather you didn't. Trust me to make the right choices."

"I would trust you with my life."

Frang clenched his jaw as a wave of emotion overtook him. Aimery had never, in the three hundred years he'd known him, said anything of the like before.

"Thank you," Frang finally managed to say.

Aimery walked out of the cottage. With his back to Frang he said, "I cannot accompany you, as much as I'd like to. You'll need to find her before Wallace and his soldiers. They'll kill her without hesitation."

"Aye," Frang said.

With a wave of the Fae's hand, a beautiful grey stallion came running out of the forest. "A gift for you to aid you in your recovery of the book. Call to me if you need me. For anything." Aimery's gaze was severe, his voice rough.

"You have my word."

And with that, the Fae commander was gone.

Frang walked to the awaiting horse and patted his neck. "You are a beauty." His gaze ran over the steed. "And built for speed. Let's see if you can catch our little thief."

He vaulted up on the horse and grabbed the reins. A smile pulled at Frang's lips when he spied the Fae knot work on the reins and halter on the horse. A glance down at the saddle showed the same artistry. He lifted the flap of the small bag attached to the saddle and found a few apples and a loaf of bread as well as a skin of water.

Once again, Aimery had made sure he was ready for anything. The smile faded as he stared off toward the east. There was only one way Kenna had known which way to go to the Druids, her power had been discovered.

How much of it, Frang didn't know. For her sake, he hoped he found her before Wallace did.

He spurred his mount into a canter as they raced after Kenna, his thoughts on catching her. And although he should be thinking of the questions he would put to her, all he could think about was crushing her soft, sweet body against his.

11

Aimery walked into his chambers to find his king waiting for him. He hesitated only a moment before he shut the door behind him.

"You aided Frang." Theron's voice was muffled and low.

"I did."

Theron turned to face him. His king's arms were crossed over his chest and his face held disappointment. "You went against my direct order."

"I did."

"You aren't going to plead your case?"

Aimery took a deep breath then shook his head. "He's a friend, Theron. After what we've done to him, I figured I owed him the horse."

"And the direction the girl took."

"Aye. That as well."

Theron sighed as his face sagged wearily. "I cannot punish you for something I would have done myself."

"And the Book of Magic?"

Theron inhaled and stood straighter, his face once more that of a king. "Frang will find the girl. What he does after that is his decision. Once that book is in his hands, he can change the tide of history."

"He won't," Aimery stated.

Theron laughed though the sound held no mirth. "I have always been amazed at how man reacts to power. We shall see how strong a man Frang truly is."

"He won't let the power influence him."

"I hope you're right."

* * *

Kenna stopped beside a stream at noon. Both she and the mare were exhausted. She had ridden a little over the years, but never for most of the day, and her day wasn't even done. Already her legs ached but she pushed aside the pain as she slid from the mare, then collapsed on the ground when her legs gave way beneath her. The mare turned her head and looked at her with soulful brown eyes.

Kenna chuckled as she patted the mare's velvety nose. "Aye, I know I'm a sight. Go drink," she said as she gave the horse a little push.

While the mare drank, Kenna slowly crawled to the water and splashed some on her neck and face before drinking in great mouthfuls. Once she'd slaked her thirst, she reached inside her satchel and took out an oatcake.

She was out in the open with no shade or cover, making her easy to spot. Too easy. With a sigh, she rose on wobbly legs and took the mare's reins to lead her to a nearby grove of trees.

Kenna sank onto a fallen log and ate while the horse munched on the sweet, green grass. How Kenna wished she had gotten the exact location of the Druids from Frang, because even though she trusted her powers to lead her in the right direction, it didn't tell her where the Druids were.

After resting, Kenna rose and mounted again, wincing at her sore muscles. "Ride like the wind," she whispered into the mare's ears, for Kenna knew her treachery would be discovered.

The Wallace would demand payment. With her life.

Unless she reached the Druids in time. She grimaced as she thought of Frang. She'd feel so much better if he were there with her, giving her his strength and his laughter.

She nudged the mare into a walk as she fingered the dagger through the material of her skirts. If only she could have trusted him with her secrets. If only he had given her some sign he wasn't after her secrets as well. She didn't know who to trust anymore.

With the heel of a hand, she rubbed her tired eyes. It was only midday, and she had much more riding to do. Already her legs ached so badly she could barely sit atop the mare, and her bottom was so sore it hurt just to think about sitting down. Yet, she had no choice.

After a deep breath, Kenna sat straighter in the saddle and pushed her pain into a dark corner of her mind. She'd deal with it later, after she found the Druids.

* * *

It didn't take long for Frang to find Kenna's trail. He urged his stallion faster. The suspicion that the Wallace and his men were gaining on him was strong, leading Frang to ride harder and faster.

The fact the horse took everything he asked without complaint, or seeming to get tired, told Frang that the stallion was most likely gifted with magic.

A smile pulled at his lips. Aimery never failed to think of things most humans wouldn't. Frang lowered himself over the grey's neck as the ground became a blur beneath him. The wind whipped at his face, drying his eyes and his lips.

When he came to a fork in the path, he pulled the grey to a stop and jumped to the ground. He squatted next to the paths, searching for signs as to which way Kenna travelled. If he chose wrong, it could very well mean her death and put the book in the Wallace's hands once again.

"I cannot allow that." Frang stood and turned to the stallion. "Do you know which way she went?"

The horse nodded his great head and nickered softly. Frang blew out a tired breath and mounted. "Take me to her."

Without hesitation the stallion continued straight, his legs nearly flying over the rough terrain of the Highlands.

* * *

Kenna shifted in the saddle again. She had slowed the mare to a walk despite the urgency that pushed her, but her body had needed the rest. Yet, with every step the mare took, pain lashed though her like lightening.

She glanced at the sun, grateful to see it sinking in the sky. It wouldn't be long before she could start looking for a place to rest for the night. Once she had some food in her, she'd put some rosemary into her water to help ease her body so she could sleep.

Suddenly, she was jerked out of her musing by her mare's sudden stop. Kenna immediately gripped the reins tighter and looked around her. She couldn't see anything, but the way her mount began to whinny and prance to the side told her there was a predator lurking nearby.

"Easy, girl," Kenna whispered to the horse and looked over the side of the narrow trail to the rocks several hundred lengths below. But no amount of calming words would ease the mare. A howl split the air, and the mare reared up.

Kenna somehow managed to keep her seat. She tried to kick the mare into a run, but the mare's wild eyes told her they wouldn't be going anywhere.

When the mare reared again, she wasn't prepared. She tried to grab onto the mare's mane, but her fingers slipped through it.

A scream tore from Kenna as she felt herself falling.

* * *

Frang jerked. "Kenna," he whispered into the fading light of day.

He leaned over the stallion, giving him a whistle that sent the horse leaping into a run. Frang knew in his heart Kenna was hurt, but how badly he couldn't guess.

In fact, he shouldn't care. But he couldn't forget the way her amber eyes had danced with laughter as he'd told her stories while they'd eaten their supper. Or how her flame red hair seemed to come alive in the sunsets.

He rounded a bend and he saw a horse slip on the narrow ledge of the mountain before regaining its footing and running off. The horse looked similar to the one he had seen Kenna ride, but if that was her horse, where was she?

Frang's stallion took the steep climb carefully, picking his way through the loose rocks that dotted the side of the mountain. Frang told himself to stay calm until he knew for sure it was Kenna's horse.

But all control left him when he spotted flame red hair amid the grey rocks. He pulled his mount to a stop and vaulted from his back.

"Kenna," he said as he rushed to her side. He swallowed when he saw how close she had come to tumbling over the side of the mountain. Blood gushed from a wound at her forehead running into her hair. Frang bent down and listened to her ragged and shallow breathing.

His gaze rose to the stallion. "Find the mare and return with her."

He didn't wait to see if the stallion did as he commanded, for he knew he would. Instead, Frang felt along Kenna's body for broken bones. He started to lift her in his arms when he heard a growl from behind him.

Frang slowly turned and saw the huge grey wolf staring at him with his teeth bared. Frang held the wolf's gaze. "Go and leave us be."

Instantly the wolf stopped growling, then he turned and loped away. With a sigh, Frang turned back to Kenna. He gently lifted her in his arms and stood.

He needed to find shelter. There were no caves to hide in for the night, nor did he have time to go down the mountain to the clumps of trees below. He looked over his shoulder at the way they had come and knew he couldn't retrace his steps.

His gaze swung to the mountain looking for anything that could shelter them. He found it in the shape of boulders. Two massive boulders served as a wall toward the trail where no one either coming or going would be able to detect them.

Frang wasted no time in hurrying toward the boulders. He laid Kenna down next to one and quickly gathered some small sticks to start a fire. Once he had the sticks gathered and arranged, he held his hands over them and closed his eyes. Within moments, the sticks caught fire.

Next, he reached under Kenna's skirts and tore a piece of her underskirt to use as a bandage for her head. He had no herbs with him and was surprised that Kenna hadn't brought any either.

He stood and walked to where he had found Kenna. He searched the area, hoping to find a small bag of herbs. Instead, he located a rather large satchel hanging gingerly on a rock over the side of the mountain.

Frang tested a rock at his left. Once he was assured of its soundness, he began his descent to the satchel. It was farther down than he'd originally thought, and more difficult to reach than he would have liked.

He was nearly to the rock that held the satchel when his feet slipped out from underneath him. Frang grabbed for anything he could as he began to fall down the mountain.

With a jerk, he came to a stop. He closed his eyes

briefly and looked up to find himself holding the satchel. Carefully, he found another foothold and once again held onto the mountain. Only then did he lift the satchel and slip the strap over his head and over one arm.

He took the climb back up as slowly as he needed to. Once he was again on the path, he rushed to Kenna, lifting the satchel over his head as he did.

A sound drew his attention, and he looked up to find his stallion had returned. With Kenna's mare.

"Thank you," he told the horse.

He opened Kenna's satchel expecting to find the Book of Magic. It filled nearly the whole satchel, and if he were to find any herbs, he needed it removed first. Frang hesitated only a moment before he gripped the heavy tome and nearly threw it on the ground beside him.

After a deep breath at the frisson of magic that ran through the book and into his fingers, he sifted through the herbs to find the ones he needed. He rose and went to the stallion, searching through the bags until he found a skin of water.

He soaked part of Kenna's underskirt with the water as he set out to stop the bleeding. It seemed to take forever for the bleeding to stop, and only then was he able to wipe away the blood that stained the side of her face and hair.

Next, he reached for the elder and put the leaf over her wound as he wrapped her head with another strip of her underskirt. As he sat back and looked Kenna over, he wasn't able to keep his fear at bay.

Fear for her safety, or fear from himself, he wasn't sure.

12

Kenna woke to her head pounding as if several hundred soldiers marched on her skull. She tried to sit up and was immediately assaulted with nausea.

"Don't move."

She stilled. She knew that voice. All too well. Slowly, she opened her eyes to find Frang staring at her, one side of him in shadow, the other illuminated by the small fire.

"You took a nasty fall," he said. "You were lucky you didn't go over the side of the mountain."

The harshness in his voice was too much. Tears stung her eyes. She turned her head away, biting the inside of her cheek to keep from crying out at the pain that simple movement caused.

She heard him move and felt his heat as he settled near her. "I'll need to check the bandages soon. You must have hit your head when you fell which caused the gash on your temple." His voice was soft and low, like a brush of velvet over her skin.

Kenna shivered and immediately he covered her with

something. She looked down to find a plaid in the colors of her clan covering her. Her gaze rose to his.

"How did you find me so quickly? The last I saw you, you were...occupied...with two women."

His gaze narrowed for just a moment before he leaned back on his haunches, his hands resting on his thighs. "So, you were at the castle last eve."

"I had to deliver the herbs to the Wallace." She wasn't able to hold his gaze and quickly looked away.

"I could have delivered them for you. But you didn't want that, did you? What is it you were trying to keep from me?"

Her eyes snapped to his. She opened her mouth to tell him all, but the accusation and distrust she saw in his gaze held her tongue.

"Thank you for saving me," she said and closed her eyes.

She heard him sigh a heartbeat before his hands gently touched her face. His touch was soothing, almost as if he took part of her pain away, though she knew that wasn't possible. Even when he removed her bandage to look at the cut, his touch was feather light.

Before she knew it, she was once again drifting off to sleep.

* * *

Frang ran a hand down his face as he stared at Kenna. She had almost told him, he had seen it in her eyes. But she must have seen something in his for she held back.

Shite!

He had been overjoyed when her eyes had fluttered open, but their amber depths had been disoriented and not the clear eyes he was used to looking into. His worry had doubled when he'd seen the amount of pain she was in.

The herbs he used weren't going to be enough. He knew that now. Yet, he had needed to know before he used his own magic on her. Frang managed to dominate many powers through his years. Though he couldn't control fire, he was able to call on its use to ignite a small flame.

Frang let his finger trail down the side of Kenna's face. She was pale and listless, unable to do more than lie there as her body tried to heal. It made Frang realize just how fragile she was, how fragile they all were.

He moved until his knees brushed against her arm, then he held his palms face down over her. Beginning at her head, he chanted the ancient words to heal her, moving from her head to her feet and back again.

Many times, he repeated the chant until he felt her body begin to heal. Once she was healed, exhaustion overtook him. Frang let himself fall to the side. He glanced at the horses before his eyes fell shut and sleep claimed him.

* * *

When Kenna opened her eyes, the pain that had crushed her last night was gone. She raised her hand and looked at it. It felt raw last eve, as if she had run it over jagged glass during her fall. Yet now, it was healed. The only evidence of the injury was faint white lines marking her palm.

"How are you feeling this morn?"

She lowered her arm and turned her head toward Frang. When no pain greeted her, she slowly began to sit up. Immediately, he was by her side, helping her.

"Don't do too much, Kenna. Your body may not be ready for it."

Only slight nausea greeted her once she was sitting up. "I'm better. Much better."

"Good." Frang's blue eyes searched hers, as if he was looking for something. He must have found it for he rose and turned away.

For several moments, she watched as he moved about their small space behind the huge boulders. She spotted the mare she'd taken from the castle and the big grey next to it. Her gaze swung back to Frang and the ease with which he moved. He was a man who moved with the grace of a cat and the lethalness of a caged beast.

Her stomach knotted with pleasure when he bent over, and she nearly saw his bum exposed. She tucked her legs under her and worked on trying to stand up.

She was nearly on her feet when the world tilted precariously. Her fingers gripped the boulder, but she couldn't find a hold to keep herself steady. She knew without a doubt she would crash to the ground, but there was nothing she could do.

Instead, Frang caught her in his arms.

His face was inches from hers. A day's growth of dark whiskers dotted his neck and face, lending him more of an air of intrigue than gruffness.

"Kenna?"

She smiled at the worry in his voice. "I cannot lie about all day."

"Jesu, Kenna." His voice was rough, but his hands were gentle as he lowered her to the ground. "I thought you were better."

Kenna chuckled. "I am better than last eve."

"But not well enough to ride."

There was something in his tone that told her he expected her to be able to ride. She raised her hand and untied the bandage around her head. Just as she expected elder had been placed on the wound.

Gently, she probed where the herb had been and only felt a slight ache when she pushed on it. She raised her eyes to Frang's. "My herbs are good, but they've never been this good. What did you do?"

He shrugged. "I soaked it in water then placed it on the wound."

Kenna shook her head, not understanding how she could have healed so quickly. If she had been completely healed, then she would have suspected magic, but there were still traces of pain in her body. So, it wasn't magic, just her herbs.

"You must have done something different. I've never healed this fast."

He smiled suddenly. "So, you've had serious head injuries before?"

A soft laugh escaped her lips. "Nay. I've cut myself before, though. I never healed overnight."

"Maybe you just weren't doing it right," he said with a wink as he once again stood.

First, he healed quickly, and now she was? Something wasn't right, and she could almost guess it had to do with Frang and not her healing skills.

Kenna opened her mouth only to hear several voices. Voices of men. Terror seized her. She grabbed hold of the boulder and tried to rise but Frang wrapped an arm around her waist to still her.

"Wait."

With that one simple word he asked the impossible. Kenna knew without a doubt that at the base of the mountain was the Wallace and his soldiers. She had to leave, to get as far away from them as possible.

She looked over her shoulder at Frang, his face was so near that his warm breath fanned her neck sending delightful shivers down her back. "I cannot."

"Wait," he said more forcefully. He gave her a gentle squeeze as he let go of her to move around the boulders.

Although every fiber of her being told her to run, she wasn't a fool. She wouldn't get to the horses without falling on her face. She closed her eyes and leaned her head against the rough surface of the boulder. Her fate was now in Frang's hands.

A moment later he was once again at her side. "'Tis Wallace. He and his men are at the base of the mountain trying to decide which way you went."

Kenna turned her head to the side and regarded her savior. "It isn't you they want, Frang. Run while you can."

"I won't leave you." He sat back against the boulders and pulled her against him. "We are hidden here. The horses are hidden. They won't find us."

"But the fire," she said only to find the fire gone and no smoke billowing toward the sky.

The only response she got was Frang's finger on her lips to keep her quiet. The fire was soon forgotten as the feel of his finger on her lips sent her blood pumping furiously. His hand covered her mouth, and then moved slowly down her chin to rest at the base of her neck.

Her eyes closed. Her heart began to beat louder, quicker. She wanted him to touch...more of her. Anywhere. It didn't matter as long as his hand was on her bare skin.

When he urged her head back against his shoulder, she acquiesced. At her back, she could feel the beat of his heart, feel his chest rise and fall with each breath he took. His hand stayed at her neck while his other wrapped around her waist just under her breasts. How she wanted his hand to cup her breasts, to run over her bare skin and ease the ache that continued to grow between her legs.

She squeezed her legs together and closed her eyes as the sensations swept over her. She was molded against him, and it was divine, but she wanted more. She wanted his kisses, his skin meeting hers. She'd dreamed of running her hands over his body, learning every inch of him.

The world he had created for her shattered when she heard horses approach. Her eyes flew open, and she started, but he held her back.

"Shhh," he whispered in her ear. "All will be well."

She had longed to trust someone and here was her chance. Her stomach clenched in fear, and the closer the horses came, the more the fear ruled her.

With the slightest of touches, Frang turned her face up to his. Trust me, his eyes seemed to beg.

And so, she did.

His head lowered. His mouth came within breaths of hers, and her breathing once again quickened. Her lips parted, and her eyes closed.

"I will protect you."

When his lips lightly brushed her ear, she sighed and settled against him. Kenna didn't know how long they sat as they did, waiting for the Wallace and his soldiers to either discover them or move away.

Finally, the Wallace commanded that they turn back where another trail forked off the main one. She smiled and slowly opened her eyes.

To find Frang watching her.

13

Frang's entire body throbbed with desire, begging him to take Kenna. She was pliant and willing in his arms. He'd seen her lips part, as if she had waited, wanting his kiss.

And the Seasons help him, he wanted to taste her sweet lips like a dying man wanted water.

His fingers moved against her throat. He'd never felt skin so soft or seen a neck so tempting. Or felt a body so inviting. He gritted his teeth to try and staunch the flow of desire through his veins, but it was futile.

He wanted her.

No longer would he deny himself, not when he had her right where he wanted her. His lips brushed across hers, tasting, testing. Her hand gripped his arm as if she were afraid he'd move away. But that one taste of her had been the sweetest of wine, and there was no turning back for him now.

He placed his lips over hers, nipping and licking until she opened her mouth and his tongue swept inside to touch hers. She moaned low in her throat when he deepened the kiss, sealing both his and Kenna's fate, for there was no turning back for him now. He would have her for his own.

As soon as he heard Wallace and his soldiers move away, he reluctantly removed his hands from Kenna's soft body and ended the kiss before he took her right then. She was still too hurt for him to make love to her as he longed to do. She opened her eyes and blinked several times as she gazed up at him with a mixture of thanks and unease.

He could well understand her disquiet. He had asked the impossible, and she had relented, trusting him when she never had before. But Frang knew that didn't mean she would trust him with everything. She feared for her life, and he had been there to defend her. Only a fool would have shunned his protection.

When she hadn't been able to stand this morning, he'd become concerned that he hadn't healed her enough the previous night. It would have been too much for him to heal her completely, though that was what he had wanted to do.

Though every fiber of his being wanted to remain in their hidden world behind the boulders, Frang knew they had to leave. Grudgingly, he helped Kenna to stand. Once she was steady on her feet, he moved to the bag he had taken off his horse the night before. He pulled out a loaf of bread and water.

"Here," he said as he handed her the items.

He could feel her eyes on him as he saddled their horses. When he turned back toward her, she was looking at her horse while she hastily ate as if it were some kind of evil creature.

"What is it?"

"Yesterday was the first time I had ridden a horse for a full day. I ached all over, and I don't think I can get back on her today."

Frang smiled. "It'll be fine. Besides, we need to make some distance on the Wallace. It won't be long before he realized this is the way we've come."

"And just where are we going?"

Her tone implied he had no inkling what she planned. He shrugged and led her mare to her. "You wanted to find the Druids, so I assumed that is where you were headed."

She gaped at him. "Do you read thoughts?"

"Nay." Though at the moment, he wanted to read hers. He waited until she had finished her part of the bread and drink then lifted her onto her mare while trying to ignore how his hands nearly spanned her tiny waist.

It wasn't until he handed her the satchel he had retrieved the day before that her eyes refused to meet his. He didn't say anything to her about the Book of Magic inside. There would be time for that later.

He kicked the evidence of their fire while he bit off some of the bread and tucked the remaining part back into his bag with the water then, swung up onto his stallion. With a nod to Kenna, he clicked the stallion into motion, leaving the safety the boulders provided them.

Frang looked down the mountain at the narrow passage and waited for Kenna. "Just in case the Wallace finds us before we make it to the bottom, you better go first."

"So, you can hold off the attack?"

He nodded.

She sighed and looked down at her hands that gripped the reins. "Surely he won't return that soon."

"I don't want to chance it."

"Aye," she whispered and set her mount in motion.

Frang followed behind her, glancing back every so often to make sure no one followed them. He knew it was only a matter of time before the Wallace found them, but he wanted Kenna safely in the Druids' Glen by then.

A pang of regret filled him. It had been nearly unbearable to leave the Glen and almost nigh impossible to stay away. Yet he had done it. Day by day he had resigned himself to the fact he would never see his beloved Glen again.

And yet, he now returned.

It seemed unfathomable.

However, there was no denying the joy that entered his soul at knowing he might catch a glimpse of the sacred Druid ground again. What he hadn't told Kenna was that he couldn't return with her. He would lead her to the edge of MacInnes land, and then the song of the Druids would call her home. It would be near impossible for him to ignore the song, but his vow to the Fae wasn't one he could ignore.

When they reached the bottom of the mountain, Kenna waited for him to come even with her. She chewed on her lower lip as if she had been thinking long and hard over something. His gaze lingered on her lips as he recalled their stolen kiss and the way it had made his blood pool in his rod.

"You haven't asked me why I left my home."

Frang smiled inwardly. "I figured you had a good enough reason for doing so."

"How did you find me?"

"I saw you riding away as I walked to the cottage." He hesitated to tell her anything more.

She licked her lips making him nearly groan with new sprung desire. "Where did you get the grey? He's a magnificent creature."

Frang leaned down and patted the stallion's neck. "That he is." He hated to lie to her, but he couldn't exactly tell her the Fae had gifted him with the horse. "I bought him."

"Bought him?" she repeated, brows raised.

Frang laughed. "Aye. Is that so surprising?"

She shook her head, her glorious red locks shining in the sun. "Just something else I didn't know about you. Don't you find it strange that you stayed with me for a week, but I don't really know anything about you?"

"Just as I don't know much about you," he countered. "I've learned that sometimes the past should be left alone."

She thought over that a moment. "I don't agree."

"Really? Please, enlighten me."

She threw him a teasing grin. "The events and decisions of the past mold a person into who he is. To truly learn about a person, you need to know his past."

Frang lifted his shoulders in a shrug. "That's one way to look at it." He felt her gaze on him, the curiosity rolling off her like fog.

"Do you have family?"

He immediately thought of Glenna, Fiona and Moira. He knew the question had been coming. In fact, he'd been waiting for it for several days. "At one time."

"Why aren't you still with them?"

He turned and looked into her amber eyes. He never tired of looking at the unusual color. "There are times when you have to do something you don't want to do. Staying wasn't an option for me. I had to leave and find a place somewhere else."

"That sounds awful. Surely there was another way than to leave. Family is important. Sometimes they are the only ones you have in the world."

Frang had to look away from her. The pain in her gaze was unbearable for him to watch. He knew how she felt being all alone. After he had been cursed, he'd had to leave his real family. Yet, he'd looked in on them every few months. Watching them grow old and die had been difficult, but not being a part of them had been the hardest thing he had ever done.

"True enough, lass," he said. He hoped she'd drop the subject, but he should have known better.

"You should return to them. If you've done something wrong, tell them you're sorry."

He fisted his hands. "Kenna, please."

Out of the corner of his eye he saw her shake her head. "Tell me why you cannot return to them."

Frang glanced over at her. "I will, just as soon as you tell me why the Wallace needed linden."

Just as he thought, she turned away, refusing to answer him. He sighed. As much as he hated her questions that made him think of things he wanted to forget, he loved the sound of her voice. Her mind was sharp and her wit quick.

He scratched his jaw. He wished he'd had a chance to shave that morning. Two days growth of beard left him itching like a daft person. All those years with a beard, and yet he couldn't stand to have whiskers now.

A large cloud covered the sun as the wind caressed his cheek like a lover's touch. If they weren't being chased by a madman intent on immortality Frang could have enjoyed the day.

He heard laughter behind him and looked over his shoulder to see Kenna lean over her mare's neck as they raced past him. Not one to pass up a challenge, Frang squeezed his legs and his stallion easily caught Kenna and her mare.

"Afraid I'll win?" she questioned.

For a moment, Frang forgot to breathe. He'd never seen her look so stunning with her long tresses flowing behind her like a red beacon and her eyes dancing with merriment. He glanced down and saw her skirts had lifted in the wind baring her legs to well above her knees.

He swallowed. Then, he met her gaze and smiled. "Afraid of losing?"

She laughed again, the sound warming the very heart inside of him. "My mare is quick."

"Aye," he hollered over the wind, "but the stallion is bigger."

"To the grove, then," she shouted before the mare leapt ahead.

Frang held back for just a moment. He watched as she raced the mare across the Scottish hills dotted with heather. She was a magnificent sight.

"Come on, lad," he whispered to the stallion. A heartbeat later the stallion stretched his legs, gaining on Kenna and the mare with every breath he took.

Just before they reached the grove of trees, he let the stallion have his head, beating Kenna and the mare by half a length.

He pulled the stallion to a stop and turned him to face Kenna. The smile she wore told him just how happy she was. She pulled the mare to a stop near him, laughing all the while. "You enjoyed that?"

"Oh, aye," she said. "I ran her yesterday, but today, well, today was different."

The only difference was that he was with her. A wealth of heat stole through his body. "What are you going to give me?"

"Give you?" she asked as she patted her mare's neck.

"For winning."

She laughed, the sound rich and robust. "What would you like?"

Frang nudged his horse near hers until they were knee to knee facing each other. "This," he said and reached for her.

14

Kenna's eyes widened in surprise as Frang pulled her against his chest and settled his lips over hers. His mouth was warm and tender as he nibbled her lips. Her hands came up to grip his shoulders as his tongue slipped into her mouth. He plundered her mouth, giving her untold amounts of pleasure.

Frang was a man who liked to kiss. He drew her closer to him, crushing her breasts against his chest as his tongue slipped through her lips and mated with hers.

When he lifted his head, she saw the desire in his eyes. But she saw something else as well—surprise.

"A most fitting prize," he said before righting her atop her mare.

Kenna waited until he turned his stallion around before she reached up and tentatively touched her lips. She could still taste him in her mouth. He tasted exotic, mystical, and powerful.

He tasted simply wonderful.

They rode in silence for hours. Kenna was lost in the kiss and her body's reaction to Frang. Her eyes never roamed far from Frang, and she kept a little behind him so she could watch him.

He rode the stallion with an ease of someone who had spent a great deal of time on a horse. But the more she learned about him, the more he confused her. He was a skilled swordsman, expert horseman and he knew herbs. In all her years, Kenna had stumbled upon a few women who recognized some herbs and their uses, but never a man.

At first, Kenna thought he might have learned from a relative. But now, she wasn't so sure. He had tried to hide it from her, but his knowledge of herbs was as extensive as hers, or better.

The fact that he not only knew of the Druids but knew their location made her hazard a guess that the Druids had taught him about herbs.

When Frang suddenly pulled up on the reins as they neared a stream, she found it difficult not to ask him the questions burning in her mind.

"We'll rest here for a bit," he said as he dismounted and led the stallion to the water.

Kenna swung her leg over the saddle and slid to the ground. After she led her mare to the water, she reached into her satchel and retrieved the loaf of bread and oatcakes she had packed.

She handed an oatcake to Frang and looked around the valley they were in. "'Tis beautiful here."

"Aye. There isn't a part of Scotland that I've seen that isn't beautiful."

"Is there one place more beautiful than any other?"

"Aye."

She waited for him to explain further, and when he didn't, she found herself disappointed. After she finished her oatcake, Frang handed her an apple.

"Where did you get these?"

He shrugged. "I bought them."

She knew he was lying. He didn't trust her enough with the truth. For all she knew, he'd probably stolen them, but at that moment, she didn't care. The apple tasted delicious.

Once the apple was gone, she drank deeply from the stream as Frang refilled their water supply. She was surprised that her legs and bottom didn't ache as they had the day before. In fact, other than a slight pain in her head, nothing hurt.

She climbed back on her mare and once again followed Frang. The more they travelled east, the more he seemed to close off from her.

* * *

Glen Wallace, laird of the Wallace clan, sat atop his horse overlooking the rolling planes of Scotland. His jaw clenched and he fisted his hand every time he thought of Kenna.

He still couldn't believe she had taken the Book of Magic. She was to have been his bride, a fitting position for one such as her. Not to mention, her skills in healing would have given him the extra knowledge he needed.

His men stood at the ready to take Kenna down with

only a word from him. Yet, Wallace found himself wondering if he wanted her dead after all. It would have been easier for him had she come to his bed willingly, but he could take her there regardless of if she was willing or not.

She still had what he needed. And wanted.

"Laird?"

Wallace turned to his first in command, Callum. "Aye?"

"Another set of tracks is now with Kenna's."

Wallace inwardly seethed. Had she found a lover? Someone to share her magic with? "It appears our little healer is no longer alone. We need to find her before she finds herself in too much danger."

"Aye, laird."

As Callum moved away, Wallace shifted in the saddle. All he desired was within his grasp. He had moved slowly with Kenna to give her time to come to grips with her new role as his bride.

Yet, she had seemed surprised at his words the night before at the castle. As if she hadn't known he'd been wooing her. Any woman in the Wallace clan would jump at the chance to be his wife. Any woman but Kenna, that is.

No one knew of his dabbling in his tower. Not even Callum who he told everything. He wanted to conquer the power, harness the magic. Then, he would show those few who would stand by his side for an eternity. He had been willing to share his gift with Kenna, but now he had other thoughts.

She would give him sons, and afterward he would toss

her aside for another woman. He would sire as many sons as he could, gifting each of them with eternity.

With a smile, Wallace nudged his horse down the hill.

"Have you changed your mind about her?" Callum asked as he rode alongside him.

"Kenna will serve her purpose. I need her."

Callum snorted. "As often as the women in the clan swoon at seeing your face, ye'll have no difficulty finding ye a woman."

Wallace looked at his friend and first in command. "I want Kenna. I will have Kenna."

"Och," Callum said, a sneer on his face. "Ye'll use her till yer done, then find another. Good plan."

"That it is," Wallace said. "I want her found before nightfall."

Each mile that brought Frang closer to the Glen made him more uneasy. Would he be strong enough not to return to the Glen? Temptation had always been a downfall of his. Kenna was a prime example.

* * *

He knew he shouldn't have kissed her, yet he'd been unable to help himself. And after that delightful taste of her, it was going to be exceedingly difficult not to kiss her again.

Or to run his hands along her soft curves.

Never before did he have to delve into his powers to keep his desires for a woman at bay, but with Kenna everything was different. Just the thought of her flaming tresses tickling his skin as she straddled his hips and rode him to ecstasy was enough to bring his rod hard and aching.

"Did I do something wrong?"

Kenna's sweet voice breaking through his vivid image of her brought him to the present. He glanced at her as she rode beside him and saw the anxious expression on her delicate features.

"Nay," he answered. "Why do you think that?"

"You've been quiet. Too quiet. Almost as if you were pensive and regretted accompanying me."

Frang chuckled. "I don't regret accompanying you, so set your mind at ease."

"But there is something bothering you, aye?"

There was no use denying it. Not now. Not when she would discover the truth in a matter of days. "Aye, there is something else."

"How close are we going to your home?"

"Very, very close." It would only be a day or two before he'd begin to hear the song of the Druids, a song only another Druid could hear to help draw them to safe territory. It would be more painful than his leaving.

Kenna cleared her throat. "Would you like to stop and visit with them? I don't have to come with you," she hurried to add.

Frang turned his head and looked at her. "That is kind of you, but I will have to decline. There are events that have taken place that I cannot change. I must stay away."

He watched as she twisted the reins in her hand. "I know you don't trust me, and I haven't given you reason to. But can't you tell me why?"

"It isn't that easy."

She held up a hand. "Nay. Don't say more. I shouldn't have asked."

When she nudged her mare into a run, Frang let her go. He had expected to live out the rest of his life without the past continuing to intrude on a daily basis. Kenna's curiosity was going to have her discover much more than if he'd just told her the truth.

He whistled to the stallion and took in the clean, Highland air as he chased Kenna. He basked in the knowledge that he wouldn't be around when she found out the truth about him. He intended to turn around as soon as she was safely on MacInnes land and find himself a nice village to call home. Many, many miles away from the Druids.

There he wouldn't have to see the accusation in Kenna's eyes for not telling her when he'd had the chance. Nor would he have to enlighten Glenna and Conall as to why he'd left in the first place.

Or explain his appearance and the curse that went with his immortality.

Nay, it was far better if he didn't go near the Druids.

Hours later, Frang led them into a small forest that skirted the base of a mountain. "We'll rest here for the night." Out of the corner of his eye he saw Kenna shiver. "It's safe enough for a fire as well."

He thought he heard her mumble a 'thank the saints.' He began to unsaddle and wipe down the horses with a handful of pine needles as she looked for wood for the fire.

Dusk was upon them, with the nightfall rapidly approaching. As soon as he finished with the horses, he looked up to find Kenna trying desperately to start the fire. He walked to her and knelt near the fire.

"Let me work at this. We'll need wood for the night."

Wearily, she stood. "I'll find some more."

Frang waited until she was out of sight before he held his hands, palm down over the wood, and coaxed a fire to life.

And then he heard the scream.

15

Kenna stared into the golden eyes of the boar and knew she was about to die. Her hand reached for her dagger beneath her skirts, but it was as if the animal knew what she did, for it growled at her.

She took a step back, her heart skidding to her feet when the animal followed. Every instinct within her told her to turn and run as fast as she could to Frang. He would be able to help her.

"Whatever you do, don't move," she heard a voice from behind her.

Kenna nodded to Frang as he moved slowly behind her. She felt his warmth moments before he brushed against her.

"Do you trust me?"

"Aye," she whispered.

"We'll never outrace him. We'll have to trick him."

Kenna was about to ask him how he planned to do that when his hand came up to rest on her waist.

"Whatever you do, don't let go of me."

She jerked her head to look at him the same time he whirled her around to crush her against his chest and roll to the ground. Kenna locked her arms around him and held on as they rolled away from the boar.

The boar shrieked its frustration as it charged after them. And then, as suddenly as Frang had set them rolling, he stopped and twisted away from her to plunge his sword into the animal.

Kenna buried her face in Frang's neck and tried to stop shaking. "I think I should have stayed at my cottage."

"You don't like your adventure?"

She shook her head. "Nay. Not the adventure, the wild animals, or the madman after me."

A sigh escaped her lips when Frang's arms came around her to give her a gentle squeeze. Suddenly, she realized how close he was to her. Body to body they lay on the ground. Her arms were still locked around him, and his eyes bore into hers. The memory of their kiss sent heat flooding her body.

Her breath locked in her throat when Frang's gaze moved to her mouth. Unwittingly, her lips parted while she waited for another kiss.

She wanted that kiss desperately.

"You'll be much happier where you're going," he whispered huskily.

She tried to swallow as his head bent toward her, but all the moisture in her body was now between her legs. Her near-death experience was long forgotten as she savored the feel of Frang's body alongside hers.

Just when she thought he would finally kiss her, he turned away and rose.

Kenna glanced at the dead boar near her and realized just how close Frang had come to getting skewered. "Thank you," she said after he helped her rise. Her body was shaking but not from her fear of the boar. It was because of Frang and what he did to her.

One side of his lips pulled up in a smile. "My pleasure, lass."

How he could be so nonchalant after almost dying was beyond her, but as long as he was with her, she felt safe.

"Go sit by the fire. I'll skin the boar and gather more wood."

Kenna shook her head. "I'll get the wood." With the desire fading, her mouth began to water as she thought of eating the roasted boar. She licked her lips and heard Frang chuckle.

She hadn't realized just how hungry she was until that moment. The travel and constant worry over the Wallace finding her had made the day long and weary. Exhaustion was pushed aside with the temptation of a hot meal and a fire to ward off the chill that had encased her soul.

Frang was a good man, a man who had risked his own life several times for her. But was that enough for her to share her secrets, her heavy burdens with him?

Nay, she thought as she turned away to start collecting wood. She would deal with her problems herself, for if she involved Frang, it would only cost him his life. And that she couldn't live with.

By the time she returned to their camp, Frang had cut off a portion of the boar and skinned it. It now roasted over the fire, its juices falling into the flames, making a loud hissing noise.

"I was getting worried," Frang said without looking at her.

She pressed her lips together, thinking quickly. "I was being more careful than before."

He knelt before the boar and rotated it on its spike to cook the other side. "I think you need to move the dagger I gave you to your hip so that it'll be easier for you to grab should you need it."

"Until the Wallace leaves me alone, I'll always need it." She squatted down and began to stack the wood within easy reach of both of them. When she sat back, Frang was regarding her silently.

"Are you ever going to tell me why the Wallace is after you?"

Kenna shook her head. "I like you."

"If you liked me, you'd trust me."

"Like and trust are two different things." She moved a fallen log closer to the fire, so she'd have something to sit on and then dusted off her hands. "If I didn't like you, I'd have already told you enough to get you killed."

Frang whistled softly. "It appears as though you are in over your pretty wee head."

"Aye, I think I am."

He crossed his arms over his chest as he leaned back against a tree and stretched his legs out in front of him. "What makes you think telling me would kill me?"

Kenna laughed. "There is nothing you could say, no trick you could use that would make me tell you anything."

"You seem rather sure of yourself."

She shrugged. "I have to be if I'm going to keep you alive."

"What about you?"

"What about me?"

"Aren't you worried about your life?"

Kenna paused as she thought over his words. She met his gaze over the fire. "Nay. My life was forfeit the moment I made my decision."

Frang's head cocked to the side. "You mean when you left your clan?"

She couldn't tell him it was when she began to suspect what the Wallace was doing with the herbs she collected. Frang was too intelligent and would figure out everything.

Instead, she simply lowered her gaze and let him believe what he would. He'd be safer that way.

When he next spoke, his voice was soft and low, barely heard over the crackling fire. "You forget, Kenna. I know where you are headed. I know what safety the Druids hold for you. Whatever you've done, they might be able to protect you for a short while, but if the Wallace truly wants you, he'll have you."

"It isn't for myself that I seek the Druids."

She could tell her words shocked him by his furrowed brow. He let his arms fall to his sides as he sat up and stared at her. "Kenna, you cannot think to turn yourself over to the Wallace willingly."

Her fingers fidgeted with her skirts, a habit she did when she was nervous. "Nay," she lied.

For a moment, she worried he wouldn't believe her. Then, he returned to his relaxed pose against the tree. "I knew you were smarter than that."

It was just like a Highlander to think his way was always the best. It was on the tip of Kenna's tongue to tell him her true plan, but she held back. There was something about Frang that told her he was much more than he led her to believe. Just what he was, she wasn't sure.

She waited until he was turning the boar again before she said, "I've been curious as to how you know so much about herbs."

His hands stilled and his sky-blue eyes rose to her face. Before the bored look he presented to the world fell over his face, she saw the hesitation and doubt in his gaze.

"Do you think only healers know of herbs?" he asked. His voice held a note of indifference, but she knew otherwise.

"'Tis true that others know of some herbs, the common herbs. Few people know of mixing herbs or what rare herbs look like."

He cut off a piece of the boar and examined it before he bit into it. "It's ready." He waited until she neared him before he said, "I will answer your question truthfully. If you answer one of mine."

Kenna hesitated. She couldn't answer just any question.

"'Tis a simple one," Frang went on as if he didn't know the quandary his comment had caused her. "My question is this. I would like for you to tell me if Brigit was a Druid."

Kenna felt the air rush from her lungs. "Why?"

He shrugged. "Is that the question you want me to answer?"

"Nay," she hurried to say. She stared at him for several long moments before she nodded. "Brigit was a Druid, or at least, she practiced their ways."

Frang cut off a piece of the boar for her, then handed it

to her. He waited until she was seated back on her log before he responded to her. "Thank you for telling me. As for your answer, I know of herbs and their uses because I was taught by the Druids."

He watched as surprise widened her eyes, and then the surprise turn into delight. "Truly? So that is why you know where they live? How you know they are still around?"

Frang smiled at her questions. Her glee was entertaining to behold. "Aye to all your questions."

"Tell me about them," she asked, her desire for information shining in her amber eyes.

Frang sunk his teeth into the boar, chewed and swallowed before he spoke. "They are very knowledgeable and powerful. Where I am taking you is the largest holding of Druids in all of Scotland. Few know of their location."

"I'll never tell," she vowed and absently bit into the meat.

"Nay, I don't think you will. Willingly."

That got her attention. She bristled as her beautiful eyes lost their luster and stared him down as if he were some nasty insect that had come to sample her food. "Nothing could make me tell."

"The Wallace could." He watched as the realization hit her. "He is a man who isn't used to losing what he wants. From what you've told me, he wants those herbs. He might be able to find someone else to collect them for him, but I think it goes deeper than that. I think he wants you."

Her eyes lowered to the ground. "He does want me. The last night at the castle, he all but proposed. I never knew he thought of me that way."

Jealousy flared to life in Frang. He couldn't imagine

Kenna with the Wallace, but Wallace was a good-looking man...and a laird. It was enough to turn many a young lass's heads.

"You could have had great power had you stayed with him." It galled Frang to even say the words. He knew he would have to let Kenna go eventually, but while she was with him, he wanted to be the center of her thoughts, as selfish as that was of him.

She shook her head, tendrils from her glorious red head falling about her face. "Never." Her gaze rose to Frang's. "He is...after something that is not his by right."

"You?"

"Nay. Something else, something that needs to be kept safe."

Frang sat forward, his food forgotten. A thrill shot through him that Kenna didn't want the laird. "Ah. You mean the book you carry in your bag?"

16

All the color drained from Kenna's face. "How…When?"

"When you fell. I knew you wouldn't leave without having some herbs. I had to remove the book to get to the herbs."

She visibly swallowed then licked her lips. "I see."

Frang decided to find out how much she would tell him. "I gather the book is of great importance to the Wallace?"

"Did you look at it?"

"Nay. I was too concerned about your wounds to worry over a book."

She relaxed and took another bite of food. She licked the juice from her lips and said, "I heard of the book from Brigit. She spoke of it as legend though, not truth. When I saw it, I knew the Wallace had to have come by it with evil in mind."

"What is the book?"

She opened her mouth then realized what she had been

about to do and promptly shut it. "Nay, Frang. I cannot tell you."

"Cannot? Or will not?"

"Both," she said sadly and turned her attention to her meal.

"I could make you tell me."

Her gaze snapped to his. "I suppose by that you mean you won't take me to the Druids?"

Frang hated to do this, but she needed to know what she was up against. "Aye."

Amber eyes shot fire at him. "You would do that? I thought you were an honorable man."

"You trust me enough to be honorable and take you to the Druids, but you don't trust me enough to tell me of the book or why you left your clan? You know nothing about me, Kenna. For all you know, I could have been hired by the Wallace himself."

She tossed the remnants of her food into the fire. "You could have, but you aren't. You aren't the type of man the Wallace would seek."

"Och, lass. You aren't understanding what I'm saying."

"I understand just fine, Frang. I'm not worldly, and I'm naïve at times, but I can sense when there is evil in someone. There is no evil in you."

With a sigh he rose to his feet. "I could have raped you by now."

"Could have but didn't. You also could have done it that first night you stayed at my cottage or the nights after. But you didn't."

He shook his head. "You're too trusting. I never told

you where we were going. I could take you far away from the Druids, and you'd never know it."

She rose and walked to him until she stood inches from him. "Will you take me to the Druids?"

He searched her amber eyes. She tried to appear calm, but deep inside he could sense her turmoil, her fear. "I'll take you to the Druids, lass."

"Will you keep me safe from the Wallace?"

"Aye." He knew what she was about now.

"Will you promise not to ask me questions about the book?"

Frang sighed loudly. "Aye."

A slow smile pulled at her lips. "I knew you were a good man."

Having her this close, seeing her full lips reminded him of their kiss, and his body exploded with desire. He fisted his hands at his side to keep from pulling her against him and tasting her again, but it took everything he had to control the nearly overwhelming desire to bury himself deep inside her and feel her sex clench around him as he brought her to orgasm.

He silently begged her to turn and go back to her place on the other side of the fire. Yet, she didn't move. Her smile dropped as her eyes roamed slowly over his face.

"Who are you?"

"Just a man."

Her hand rose up and gently cupped his cheek. "Nay, I think not. There is more to you than you are telling me, but I can hardly fault you for keeping your secrets when I keep my own."

"I don't want to know your secrets right now."

"Oh? Then what do you want?"

She shouldn't have asked, and he shouldn't have goaded her into it. But Frang couldn't help himself when he was around her.

"This," he said as he pulled her against him and slanted his mouth over hers. With one hand he supported the back of her head, the other he moved to the small of her back.

He nipped at her lips, begging her to open for him the same time he prayed she'd push him away. She was intoxicating, seductive and oh, so alluring.

Instead of pushing him away, she wrapped her arms around his neck and buried her fingers in his hair. Frang moaned and pulled her tighter against him. Her lips parted, and he stroked her tongue with his.

He could get drunk off her lips. Already his head swam with images of him baring her breasts so he could feast on them. Desire engulfed him, need consumed him.

Kenna floated on a cloud of contentment. Each touch of Frang's tongue sent her spiraling into an abyss of pleasure, each breath she took brought her more desire, more heat. Her breasts tingled, her stomach clenched in anticipation and a strange, intense pressure began between her legs.

His dark locks were thick and soft between her fingers. His arms were like iron as they locked around her, holding her to him, making her feel every hard inch of him all the way down her body.

His hands moved over her back, her hips, her waist... and her breasts. She sucked in a breath and arched into his hand as Frang cupped her breast.

When his finger grazed her nipple, a startled cry

wrenched from her lips as she broke their kiss. Her body shook with passion and the fierce desire Frang called from within her.

She opened her eyes to find him gazing at her. His normally bright eyes had darkened, the desire there for anyone to see. He was holding nothing back from her.

A sane woman would step away and break the hold he had on her. But when it came to Frang, Kenna was anything but sane. The man had the uncanny ability to know her deepest thoughts, touching her soul as no one ever had.

Her eyes closed on a moan as his finger teased her sensitive nipple.

"You like that."

She smiled at his statement. "You know I do. Your hands are like magic."

"There's no magic here, Kenna," he said as he nuzzled her exposed neck. "I am only a man who sees something he wants."

Her stomach somersaulted at his words. She ran her hands over his wide shoulders and muscular arms while she drifted in the sea of pleasure.

To her disappointment, she felt him pulling away. Slowly, but surely, he stepped away from her until only their hands touched.

"Forgive me," he said. "I should be able to control my own passion."

Kenna's heart thudded. She hadn't wanted him to stop. Had he laid her down on the ground, she would have succumbed to him. Gladly.

She released his hand and took a step away from him.

With difficulty, she swallowed and turned her back to him. Her legs barely supported her as she leisurely made her way back to the log. It was going to be near impossible for her to sleep with her body raging as it was.

Though she wanted to curse Frang, she couldn't, not after he had awoken her desires as he had.

* * *

Frang awoke before dawn, his thoughts jumbled and his mood dark. He rose to stretch and found himself walking toward Kenna. He knelt beside her and watched her sleep. She looked so beautiful and peaceful that he found it difficult to breathe. He recalled her lithe form in his arms and how she had responded to his slightest touch.

He could have taken her last night, but he would have taken advantage of her, and he couldn't do that. He might not know how guilty she was in helping the Wallace, but she still deserved more than a wild rutting on the ground.

Because that was exactly what it would have been. Frang had nearly lost his control over his desires. He had hung on by an unraveling thread, and he'd had to use magic to pull away from her.

Even now, staring at her, he had the urge to lean down and kiss her awake, to stretch out beside her and pull her against him.

"By all that's magical, let me get her to the Glen quickly," he whispered.

Kenna stirred then stilled. He rose once more and focused his Druid powers within him. Then, when the magic was pulsing inside him, he spread his arms wide to determine how close the Wallace and his men were.

Frang's eyes flew open as his arms dropped. Shite! They were close, too close. He pivoted and rushed to Kenna. "Kenna. Wake up. We must get moving."

Her eyes opened to look at him. She blinked then sat up groggily. "What is it?"

"The Wallace is closer than I thought. We need to get moving. If we ride hard, we might make it to MacInnes land by nightfall."

She jumped up, all sleepiness gone as she readied herself and her bag while Frang saddled the horses. Once both horses were prepared, he helped her mount, and with one last look over his shoulder, he nudged the grey into a gallop.

Fear urged him faster, but he held back, not wanting to tire the horses when they had so many leagues to cover in one day.

"Frang."

He looked over his shoulder and slowed the stallion so Kenna could catch up with him. "Aye?"

"How close is the Wallace?"

He sighed. "Closer than I would like. Much closer than I'd hoped."

"Did you see him?"

In a manner of speaking. He turned his head straight and nodded, praying she wouldn't ask more questions.

"I'm not going to make it to the Druids, am I?"

He glanced at her before he reached over and took her hand in his. "Aye, Kenna. You will. I gave you a vow, and I'll see it done."

She gave him a weak smile of gratitude. Reluctantly, Frang released her hand and concentrated on the road before them. He didn't like seeing the panic in her beautiful amber eyes. He much preferred the passion.

Out of the corner of his eye, he saw something flash. Frang, he heard Aimery call in his head.

Without a second's hesitation, he steered them off the road and across the grassy hillside.

"There's no cover," Kenna exclaimed.

"We had none on the road either. We're less likely to encounter anyone off the road, and we'll travel faster."

He hoped he wasn't lying to her. Aimery had a good reason for sending them onto the hillside rather than the road.

Frang's gaze slid to the satchel that hung around Kenna and held the Book of Magic. It would only take one spell from the book to have them transported to the Glen in a blink.

But the consequences would be severe.

* * *

Glenna MacInnes screamed as she bolted upright in bed.

"What is it?" her husband, Conall, asked as he sat up and placed a hand on her back.

Her hands shook as she pushed her hair off her sweat-soaked face. "'Tis Frang."

"Frang?" Conall had woken fully, his attention alert. "What about him?"

Glenna turned to face her husband. "He's returning."

Conall's gaze searched hers in the moonlit chamber.

"By the saints," he whispered with dread. "You've had a vision."

"Aye."

He stood and lit a candle, then he returned to the bed and took her hands in his. "What was it? Tell me every detail."

As one of the Druids in an ancient prophecy, Glenna had powers bestowed on her by the Fae. She could control fire, and in addition, she had visions. Every vision she had ever had had come to pass.

She licked her lips, not knowing where to start. "The Frang I saw isn't the Frang we knew."

"Make sense, love." Conall's brow furrowed deeply.

"The Frang I saw in my vision was young with dark hair. And he was wearing a plaid."

Conall's silver eyes sharpened. "Did you recognize the plaid?"

"It looks like either a MacDonald or a Malcolm plaid. It was hard to tell."

He waved her on. "What else?"

"He was with him a woman with flame red hair, and they were riding hard. To us."

Conall nodded. "They are being pursued?"

"Aye. I sense great urgency and fear in Frang, but not for himself, for the woman. It was very important to him that they reach our land for her." She reached out and placed her hand on her husband's arm. "Conall, she's a Druid."

Her husband's eyes closed as he let out a breath. When he opened his eyes, they held the calculating part of her husband that ruled his clan and kept the Druids safe.

"Always before your visions have occurred in the present. Not in the past."

"I don't think this vision is of the past. The Frang I saw was thinking of us."

Conall rose and paced the front of their bed. Glenna smiled at his warrior body bared for her to gaze upon.

"That's impossible," he said.

Glenna clucked her tongue at him. "You of all people should know that you shouldn't say that. After everything we've seen, and everything we've been a part of, you know anything is possible."

"Frang is an old man. Have you forgotten the long white beard and long white hair?"

"Nay, but I always told you Frang might look old, but one look into his eyes and I saw youth there."

He stopped pacing and leaned on the foot of the bed. "That would mean that Frang disguised himself while he was here."

"Aye. It could also mean that he's immortal."

Conall snorted. "Frang is a man, just like I am. He's not immortal."

"Dartayous is. Or have you forgotten?" she asked with a smile.

Conall's lips flattened. "Your brother-in-law is half Fae, that doesn't count."

"Yet you've told me before that Frang has never aged as long as you've known him. When I asked him how long he had been at the Glen, he never gave me a direct answer."

"He never gave anyone a direct answer," Conall grumbled.

Glenna scooted off the bed and walked to her husband. "Regardless, I think we better prepare for Frang's arrival."

"What is after him?"

She looked into Conall's silver gaze. "A powerful man who's bent on evil."

17

Kenna could barely keep her eyes open. They had ridden all day, stopping only to rest the horses for brief periods. Her steed stumbled and Kenna gripped the reins and the mare's mane in panic.

Frang pull up ahead of her as he waited. "Everything all right?"

"Aye." She patted the mare's neck. "She's tired."

"We all are." She heard the weariness in Frang's voice, though he kept his face impassive.

They rode together for a distance before she asked, "We didn't reach MacInnes' land, did we?"

Frang looked out at the sinking sun and shook his head. "Nay, we didn't."

She didn't like the pang of dread that crept into her soul at Frang's soft words. She looked over her shoulder but saw no one following them, and no sign that the Wallace and his men had caught them.

"They're there, Kenna. Do not doubt it."

She turned her head to Frang. "What aren't you telling me?"

He sighed. It was getting harder and harder to ride toward the Glen. Already he could hear the Druids' call. It was faint, but he could hear it. It called to his soul to return home.

A soft hand touched his arm. "We're close to your family, aren't we?"

He didn't question how she had known only nodded.

"Frang, I'm so sorry."

"Don't worry over me, Kenna. You aren't safe yet."

"But I don't see them," she argued.

Frang fingered the hilt of the dagger at his waist. "I can feel him."

Kenna shuddered. "How far are we from MacInnes land?"

"Several hours."

"But you know this land, don't you? The Wallace doesn't. Surely you know a way to get me there quickly."

He looked at Kenna, her face bathed in the orange light of the setting sun. Frang most certainly knew a way. He glanced at the sinking sun, then over his shoulder before turning back to Kenna.

She looked ready to fall out of the saddle, and her steed didn't look much better. Frang patted the mare's neck, giving some of his energy to the horse. Immediately, the mare's head picked up.

Frang smiled inwardly before he glanced at Kenna. "We'll have to ride fast."

"I ken." She opened her mouth to say something then

stopped and tilted her head to the side. "Do you hear that?" she whispered.

"What?"

"Singing. Beautiful singing."

Frang did smile then. "Come, Kenna. Your destiny awaits," he said then nudged the stallion into a run.

He held his horse back so Kenna and her mare could keep up. He could feel the Wallace closing in on them, as if magic aided him in their capture.

Frang glanced over his shoulder often to check on Kenna, and it was during one of those looks as they crested a hill that he saw them.

Kenna's mare stumbled again and slowed. Frang turned the stallion around and raced back to her.

He reached for her. "Come, Kenna. Your mare can go no farther."

"Your horse cannot carry two."

Frang pulled her off her mare. "He can." He settled Kenna behind him and once her arms were secured around his waist, he squeezed his knees and the stallion leapt into a run.

* * *

"Conall," Glenna hollered as she ran along the battlements.

He poked his head out of the gatehouse. "I'm here."

"Your men," she panted. "Get them ready."

His head turned to look out over his land. Behind him was the forest and to his left the loch. "They're coming."

"Aye," she said, her breathing more even. "Now.

Conall, the man after them has a score of men with him. And they're gaining on Frang."

Conall's silver gaze swung back to her. "Magic?"

"I think so."

"We're going to need more help. Get the Druids to the cliff. I'll get my men ready."

She reached out a hand to stop him then rose up on her tiptoes to place a kiss on his mouth. "Be careful."

He grinned devilishly. "With a wife that can control fire, I'll be fine."

The smile faded from Glenna's face as she looked to the forest where the Druids had hidden for centuries. Their leader was returning.

She raced down the stairs, through the bailey to the entrance of the cave that would lead her to the Druids. A shiver passed through her body as she spied a spider scurrying for cover.

"You'd best get out of the way," she said as she rushed past it. As she ran through the dark, twisting caves, torches lit before she reached them then faded as she ran past. Every time she ventured into the caves, she thanked Conall for installing the torches for her.

Before she reached the entrance to the stone circle the Druids called home, she could feel Frang draw closer. She lifted her skirts higher and lengthened her legs.

"Glenna," Malina, one of the Druids, called as she ran into the stones.

"Malina, I need everyone on the cliff. Now," she said.

Glenna didn't wait for the other Druids as she walked to the cliff. It was not only where she'd married, but it was where they had defeated the man who had killed her parents and kidnapped her. It was the place where she had welcomed her powers and used them fully for the first time.

She had no doubt she would be using them this night.

Her gaze shifted to the setting sun. Night was nearly upon them. Only a thin slit of the sun remained, and then the land would be cloaked in darkness.

"Why have you called us?" Malina asked as she came to stand beside Glenna.

Glenna looked over at the priestess with her long flowing raven tresses and smiled. Malina had tried her best to rule the Druids, but all of them missed Frang. Malina refused to accept the High Priestess position until all the Druids agreed to her as their high priestess.

"Frang has returned."

Malina's dark gaze searched hers. "Is he in danger?"

"Aye." Glenna watched Malina's beautiful face line with worry.

Malina nodded. "We will be ready to protect him."

Glenna wondered if she should prepare the other Druids for Frang's arrival. She forgot about telling them anything as she spotted her husband and his men sneaking from the castle to protect Frang.

"They've shut and locked the gate," Malina said. Her gaze returned to Glenna's. "It is a great evil, then?"

Glenna nodded. "An evil bent on capturing Frang." And the woman with him, she added silently.

* * *

"Frang," Kenna screamed.

He knew what she saw. The Wallace. Frang bent low

over the stallion and prayed they'd reached MacInnes land in time.

"Hang on, Kenna," he shouted over his shoulder as the stallion gave a quick burst of speed.

They were very near Conall's land. The Druids' call was nearly deafening now, and he knew Kenna heard it as well. His plan to leave her at the border of the MacInnes now would no longer work. Which meant he'd most likely have to face Conall and Glenna. He desperately wanted to see them, he just didn't want to answer the questions he knew they'd ask.

Kenna's hold tightened on him. He chanced a glance over his shoulder and saw how quickly the Wallace had gained on them. They weren't going to make it.

A cry of rage tore from Frang. He had never broken a vow before in his life, and he refused to do so now.

Just as he was opening his mouth to call to Aimery, he saw something ahead in the growing darkness. It looked like a man, aiming an arrow. But not at him.

Frang smiled.

Then Kenna screamed and jerked to the left. Frang reached back for her at the same time he saw one of Wallace's men grab for her. An instant later, the soldier screamed and fell off his horse, an arrow in his chest.

Two heartbeats later they crossed onto MacInnes land, but Frang didn't slow despite the magic he felt coming from atop the cliff. He continued deep into the forest for the one place he knew he had to bring Kenna—the only place she'd truly be safe.

Behind them he heard screams and shouts as their pursuers were stopped by Conall's men and Druid magic.

Frang guided the horse through the forest, and when they came to the nemeton, he slowed then stopped the horse.

He raised his head to the cliff where he knew Glenna would be. Kenna sucked in a startled breath when fire shot from Glenna's hands and encircled the Wallace soldiers.

"Who...what is that?"

Frang chuckled. "That is Glenna, wife to the laird of the MacInnes. She's a very powerful Druid."

"I didn't know Druids had that kind of magic."

He dismounted and reached for Kenna. He took the stallion's reins and began walking through the forest. "Most Druids do not hold that kind of power. Glenna and her two sisters were part of an ancient prophecy and because of that were given special powers."

"Given?" she questioned as she fell into step beside him.

Frang cursed himself as ten kinds of fool for letting that bit of information slip. He was just so relieved to have Kenna on Conall's land.

"'Tis not my place to tell you," he finally answered. "The Druids will be able to answer most of your questions."

She stopped and put her hand on his arm. Slowly, he turned to face her. Even in the darkness, he knew there would be doubt and anger in her beautiful amber gaze.

"Yet, you know the answer."

He nodded, knowing what her next question would be.

"How?" Her tone was low, yet it held a touch of hysteria.

Frang turned away from her and continued walking. "It doesn't matter how, Kenna. I just do."

"You don't trust me enough to tell me."

"There never has been that kind of trust between us. You have your secrets, I have mine."

"And if I was willing to share mine? Would you tell me yours?"

Frang closed his eyes and sighed. "Keep your secrets." He didn't like the pain that pierced his chest as he let the words slip through his lips. How many secrets had he kept in his three hundred years of immortality? Too many to count, and he had brought Kenna to the Druids, a sacred place for which he would die rather than to give away the location to the enemy. Yet, Kenna didn't trust him enough to share a part of herself with him.

They walked in silence through the dark forest. Frang could have found his way with his eyes closed he knew the forest so well, but he treaded slowly for Kenna's sake. Several times she tripped over roots or stumbled over fallen limbs, and each time Frang caught her. And each time, she hastily pulled away from him.

When he finally saw the stones, a smile pulled at his lips. He had forgotten their beauty in the five years since he had left. Magic pulsed from the rocks and the song of the Druids flowed around him like a sea of tranquility.

"You hear it, don't you?" Kenna whispered.

"Aye."

She started forward then halted and turned to him. "They are in the stones?"

"The stone circle keeps the Druids hidden from all who would seek them. Only those who truly believe are able to see the stones."

She laughed and turned back to the stones. "I'm frightened."

"Don't be." Frang took a quiet step back. "Go on, Kenna. They await you."

For each step she took toward the stones, Frang took a step back. He wanted her inside the stones and surrounded by the Druids so he could make his escape. If he was lucky, he'd be off Conall's land before the laird found him.

Frang smiled through the sadness as Kenna stepped between the stones. She was gone from him now, forever lost to the Druids. He should be excited that she had found her calling, but all he could feel was the deep pain in his chest at her no longer beside him.

It was time for him to go, though he found it harder and harder to make himself leave her. He reached up and grabbed the grey's mane to mount when a familiar voice stopped him.

"You don't really think I'm going to let you leave without talking first, do you?"

18

Frang sighed and turned to face Conall. The laird of the MacInnes had been leaning against a tree. He pushed off the tree and walked toward Frang.

"Glenna had a vision that you would be coming here. She said someone chased you."

He should have known Glenna would have one of her visions. Had she seen him as he was? Or did they still think him the old man he had shown the world for three hundred years. "Glenn Wallace is his name. He's laird of the Wallace clan and dabbling in magic."

Conall nodded, the darkness hiding his face. "Let's return to the castle, Frang. There are many questions I need answers to."

"I cannot," Frang said and mounted. "Please understand, Conall. It was never my intention to return. But I had no choice."

Conall moved until he stood next to the stallion and petted the animal. "I gather you speak of the woman?"

"Aye." Frang looked over his shoulder trying to calculate if he could make it off MacInnes land.

"Don't even try it," Conall warned. "You owe me a few moments, Frang. After all, I am now protecting the woman."

Frang cursed long and low. "All right, but I'm not going to the castle. We can talk here."

Conall turned on his heel. "Nay. We talk at the castle, or I release the woman to the Wallace."

"That's an empty threat, Conall," Frang called.

But he couldn't take the chance. He clicked to his horse and followed Conall to the cave entrance that led deep into the mountain and then into the bailey of MacInnes Castle.

He stopped at the entrance and dismounted. Conall stood with his arms crossed over his chest, the light of the torches illuminating his face.

"You won't turn Kenna over to the Wallace."

Conall shook his head. "I'd never turn a Druid over to evil."

"Then talk here. I need to leave."

"Why?" Conall asked. "Why the hurry to leave your home?"

Frang looked away. "You don't understand, Conall. I had to leave."

"With no word to us or the Druids?" Conall's voice had turned hard and cold.

Frang didn't blame him though. "Sometimes we aren't given a choice."

"There is always a choice."

He turned to look at Conall and saw the anger radiating from the laird. "I've missed you, too."

Conall snorted and rolled his eyes as his arms dropped and he turned away. He'd gone only two steps before he pivoted and returned to Frang. "What you did was wrong, Frang. Many people counted on you."

"I know."

"Is that all you can say?" Conall bellowed.

Frang took a deep breath. "I thought you had questions for me."

"That's when I actually thought you might answer them," Conall retorted furiously.

"If I'm able to answer, I will." Frang hated that Conall couldn't see past his own anger to the truth.

"Shite. I don't believe you."

Frang turned to leave and spotted Glenna. She stared at him with her golden-brown eyes as if she had seen a ghost. Without a word she flew into his arms. Frang hugged her to him, welcoming the warmth and friendship she offered him.

She pulled back and searched his eyes. Gently, her hand came up to touch his face. "If it wasn't for your eyes, I wouldn't know it was you."

He smiled down at her. "Ah, 'tis good to see you again, Glenna."

"We've missed you."

Frang glanced at a glowering Conall. "I don't think all of you did."

She tsked and waved away his words. "Don't pay Conall any mind. He's angry, and you know how he is when he's angry." She started to pull him into the cave, but he stopped her. She turned back to him. "What is it?"

"He cannot stay," Conall answered for him.

Glenna looked from Conall to Frang. "What is he talking about?" she asked Frang.

He sighed and tugged his arm free of her hold. "Just as Conall said. I cannot stay."

"But you've only just arrived and under attack I might add. You look as though you've been traveling for days. I'd say you need rest, food, and sleep."

Frang shook his head sadly. "It won't be here, Glenna, as much as I'd like it otherwise."

"You'd leave without seeing the Druids? Without giving us reasons for your leaving in the first place? Without saying goodbye to the woman you brought?"

Frang clenched his jaw as he thought about Kenna. He couldn't say farewell to her, it would hurt too much. He looked away from Glenna. "I was never supposed to return. You have no idea how hard this is on me."

Conall strode toward him. "Then why did you come back?"

Out of the corner of his eye, Frang saw Glenna place a hand on her husband's arm. "Because of the woman," Glenna said. "Sometimes you can be so dense for such a smart man."

Frang met Conall's gaze and waited. "Protect Kenna. She was only taught the basics of being a Druid, but she has a natural talent for healing. With training, she'll be a great asset."

Slowly Conall nodded. "You know I'll protect her with my life. Does she know who you are?"

Frang shook his head. "Wait until I'm gone before you tell her."

"Hell, I don't know what to tell her," Conall shouted.

"All my life you looked...well, not as you are now. What happened, Frang?"

"It was a curse," he answered. "It was fulfilled with the prophecy, and I was freed from its bonds."

Glenna's eyes filled with tears. "Did no one know?"

"Nay," Frang said. "Only Aimery. None of you were ever supposed to discover the truth."

Conall clasped his shoulder. "Stay with us. Whatever you are now, you are still a Druid. They need a leader."

"They have a leader," he said and looked to Glenna. "One more thing," he said as he turned and grabbed the grey's reins. "Kenna has something with her that needs to be destroyed. See that it gets done immediately. Kenna won't want to part with it, but Aimery will make her understand why she needs to hand it over."

"What is it?" Glenna asked.

Frang didn't even want to say the words out loud. "It's a book, a very important book that doesn't need to be lying about for any man to get his hands on it."

He mounted and turned the grey to leave and found Kenna standing in the way.

Kenna's stomach was in knots, knots that fell to her feet like lead. She hadn't meant to eavesdrop on Frang's conversation, but she hadn't been able to tell them she was there after hearing he had returned to his home.

His eyes widened in surprise before he hid behind a mask of indifference. "You're safe. Just as I promised."

"You were going to leave without saying farewell."

"It's for the best."

"For whom?" she asked. "You? I didn't even get to thank you."

Frang inclined his head slightly. "You've done so now."

Inside, she seethed with hurt and anger. The man before her wasn't the same man who had risked his life several times on their journey. The man before her was a stranger. "Godspeed then," she said and turned to leave.

The happiness she had felt at finding the Druids was gone, leaving a festering wound in her chest that no amount of herbs would ever heal. She hadn't expected to hurt at Frang's departure, but then again, she had at least expected him to say goodbye to her, not leave her so unexpectedly.

She stumbled through the forest trying to find her way back to the stones when gentle hands took her shoulders to steady her. She looked to her left and found the beautiful woman she had seen in Frang's arms. She didn't like the jealousy she'd felt at seeing Frang touch another woman.

"Easy," the woman said. "All will be well."

"Nay," Kenna said and blinked back tears.

The woman ran her hand up and down Kenna's arm. "You're exhausted, Kenna, and very emotional. 'Tis natural to feel as you do."

Kenna stopped and faced the woman. "You know my name?"

The woman smiled. "Aye. Frang told me. Forgive me," she said. "I am Glenna MacInnes, wife to Laird Conall MacInnes."

"My lady," Kenna said.

Glenna laughed. "Nonsense. Call me Glenna. Now, why don't you tell me how you met Frang?"

Frang sat atop the horse and stared at the spot where Kenna had been. He should leave, he knew, but he found himself unable to do so.

"Come have a drink," Conall called from behind him. "You can leave afterwards."

Still, Frang didn't move. The hurt he had seen in Kenna's eyes was like a dagger to his heart. He knew leaving her was going to be difficult, but he had expected her to be occupied with the Druids and not notice his absence until he was gone.

"Frang," Conall called.

He blew out a breath and kicked free of the stirrups before dismounting. He took the grey's reins and followed Conall through the maze of caves until they reached the bailey. Once there, he handed over the grey to a stable lad.

"Feed him well, lad. He deserves it," Frang said before he followed Conall into the castle.

Frang looked around the great hall noting little changes here and there. A few more tapestries hung on the walls, but overall, the castle still beckoned to him like a long lost love.

Conall sat in his chair before the hearth and poured two tall goblets of ale. He handed one to Frang and lifted his to his mouth. Frang drank heavily, letting the intoxicating liquid pool in his belly.

"I'd never expected a woman would be the reason you'd returned," Conall said after a long stretch of silence.

Frang lowered himself into the chair opposite Conall and shrugged. "I'd never expected to see the Glen again."

"You knew this and still you left?"

"Aye."

Conall shook his head. "Why?"

"When you are cursed by the Fae, you do what you are told."

"How long have you been cursed?"

Frang let his head drop back against the chair as he gazed at the crossed swords above the hearth. "Three hundred years."

"Shite. Are you immortal?"

Frang laughed. "Not anymore. That was lifted with the curse."

"Are you sure?"

His gaze moved to Conall to find the laird watching him intently with his silver eyes. "I haven't tested it, if that's what you mean." As soon as the words were out of his mouth, he remembered the wound on his arm and how fast it had healed at Kenna's cottage.

"What are your plans now?"

Frang hadn't thought past entrusting Kenna to the Druids. "I don't know."

"The Wallace and his men are gone, but I have no doubt they'll return."

Frang straightened in his chair. "I'd assumed that once he realized she was with the Druids, he'd leave her alone. Yet, I was a fool. He has no idea Druids are here. He'll keep coming after her until he has her. And the book."

"He nearly caught you. Had I not had my men at the ready, you'd be dead, and he'd be on his way back to his castle with Kenna."

Frang ran a hand down his face and sighed. He had never been wearier in his life. "Aye. He gained on us quickly. Too quickly."

"Magic?" Conall asked.

"I think so."

"Why does he want Kenna so desperately?"

Frang leaned his elbows on his knees. "He's looking for immortality, and with Kenna's knowledge of herbs, he almost achieved it."

"Surely not with just herbs alone."

Frang shook his head. "Nay. He had the Book of Magic."

"By the saints," Conall exclaimed, his silver eyes flashing. "I thought that book was just legend."

"All legends start somewhere."

"But you said *had*."

Frang laughed. "Kenna took it from him."

Conall's face drained of color. "She has it with her?"

Frang nodded.

"My God, Frang," Conall said as he rose to his feet. "I knew the Wallace had left too quickly and without a fight, and now I know why. He knows where Kenna and the book are. He'll return with more men."

Frang let his head sag forward. There would be no leaving for him now. Conall and the Druids would need him. And more importantly, Kenna would need him.

Damn.

19

Kenna woke slowly and stretched. It felt good to sleep in a bed again. She hadn't wanted to take Glenna's offer to sleep in the castle, but she wasn't able to dissuade her. Glenna could be most persuasive.

At first Kenna hadn't wanted to leave the Druids and the stone circle, but knowing it was within walking distance from the castle had put her at ease.

The Druids she had met were just as she expected. They were almost ethereal and enchanting. Their magic flowed around them like the sea, strong and true. She couldn't wait to return to the stones and begin her learning.

Yet, there was one thing that dampened her spirits. Frang's leaving. She couldn't believe he had left and had intended to do so without saying anything to her.

The anger that she had worked so diligently to expel the night before swarmed her again. She shoved aside the blankets, swung her legs over the side of the bed and rose. She walked to the narrow window and looked out over the land.

Since she had arrived at MacInnes castle in the dead of night, she hadn't seen much of it and was eager to explore. Her gaze wandered over the rolling hills that surrounded the castle, the thick forest, and loch. Though she couldn't see it from her vantage point, she knew there was a cliff and a mountain to the side.

A knock sounded on her door interrupting her gazing. When she opened it, she found a smiling Glenna standing before her. In the daylight, Glenna was even more beautiful with her brunette hair and golden-brown eyes.

"Did you sleep well?"

"I did. I didn't realize just how much I missed sleeping in a bed until last night," Kenna said with a laugh.

Kenna stepped to the side to allow Glenna inside, and that's when Kenna saw the servants behind her. She turned to look at Glenna.

"I thought you might like a bath," Glenna said as she motioned the servants to set the large wooden tub before the hearth.

Kenna licked her lips in anticipation while watching bucket upon bucket of water being emptied in the tub. "Oh, aye. Very much so."

"Take your time," Glenna said and walked to the door. "I'll be waiting for you in the great hall."

Kenna couldn't wait to be alone and sink into the tub. Steam rose from the water, beckoning her and her tired muscles. As soon as the last servant left her chamber, she shut the door and quickly discarded her clothes.

She stepped into the tub and sighed. As she lowered herself into the water, she began to unbraid her hair, letting the red strands leisurely float around her.

She leaned her head back against the tub as she let her muscles relax and her mind drift. Immediately she thought of Frang and his kisses, his soft lips and the way they felt against her skin. Her eyes closed as she recalled the way his mouth moved over hers and how his hands knew just where to touch her to bring her the most pleasure. She wanted to know more of the glorious feelings he aroused in her, to explore the desire she felt when he was near. She had seen couples mate before and knew Frang's cock would pierce her.

Her breathing grew ragged as she thought of seeing him naked, of stroking his rod in her hands. Instantly her body heated, her breasts swelled, and the ache began between her legs. She clenched her jaw angrily and opened her eyes as she sat up and began to wash.

It grated on her nerves that she couldn't stop thinking of Frang. What made it even worse was that, apparently, he had no problem forgetting about her, evidenced by his hasty exit.

She put her face in her hands and took a deep breath. She had to face the fact she had become attached to Frang because he had been her savior, the one man that had put his life in danger for her. And the only man that hadn't begged to hear her secrets.

Her mind filled with snippets of conversations with Frang. She found it hard to focus on anything other than him, and just when she thought she couldn't take it anymore, she heard the song of the Druids.

The soft melody at once calmed her crowded mind and soothed her body. She picked up the bar of soap that floated in the water and once more set out to washing herself and her hair.

By the time she rinsed and stood to dry off, Kenna was able to set aside any anger she felt for Frang. He had his own secrets, ones that had kept him from his home for five years. Though she wished he had stayed, she tried to bear in mind he had no choice but to leave.

Kenna reached for her gown that she had left on the hooks the night before only to find it gone and another one in its place. She looked around the chamber to make sure no one had snuck in then touched the soft cream gown.

It was of plain design, but she liked it that way. She hurried to pull on the gown. The fit was nearly perfect. It was a little snug across her breasts, but it wasn't noticeable. Her gaze moved to the Wallace plaid she had worn all her life, a plaid that she would no longer wear. Kenna wondered if she would ever wear a plaid again. A few of the Druids wore the MacInnes tartan, but most went without anything.

And so would she.

Kenna, satisfied with her decision, reached for the comb atop the chest at the foot of the bed. It had felt wonderful to wash her hair, though it would take hours for it to fully dry because of its thickness. Not only was her hair thick, but it tangled easily. She had tried to keep it plaited during her journey here, but it was stubborn and often came out of its braid.

Kenna was so intent on combing out the tangles she never heard her door open.

Frang leaned against the door and watched as Kenna pulled the comb through her long-wet tresses. Many times, he'd wanted to run his fingers through the length, almost as many times as he'd wanted to kiss her.

He wasn't sure why he had come other than he had wanted to see her, to know she was happy and safe. Now, as he stared at her, he wasn't sure what he would say. She was most likely still angry and had every right to be.

Suddenly, her gaze shifted to him. She stilled as they stared at each other across the chamber. Frang took a deep breath and straightened from the door.

"You're still here."

Her voice gave no notion whether she was angry or pleased with that fact. And that worried Frang.

He nodded. "It seems as though I won't be leaving for some time."

"Why?"

This was why he hadn't wanted to speak to her. He couldn't tell her everything. Not yet, maybe not ever. "I need to be sure the Wallace won't return for you."

She set aside her comb and moved her hair off her shoulder to trail down her back in a long red wave. "Do you think he will?"

"I know that we cannot discount that he might."

She turned away with a sigh. "It seems that our secrets once again keep us separated."

Frang stepped into the chamber and closed the door behind him. "Secrets have a way of revealing themselves with time. Just as one of my secrets was overheard by you last eve."

"Aye," she said and moved to the window. "I did overhear a secret. This had been your home. That is how you knew of the Druids, but what it doesn't explain is why you left in the first place." She turned to look at him. "Is that one secret you won't share with me?"

He moved to sit on the chest at the foot of the bed and raked a hand through his hair. "I'm tired of secrets, Kenna. I'll tell you everything but be prepared to hear the answers."

She nodded and walked to him, then knelt before him. "How do you know about the herbs?"

"I'm a Druid. For a time, I was the High Priest here." He licked his lips, trying to ignore the swelling of his rod at having Kenna betwixt his legs.

Her mouth opened in surprise. "Why did you never tell me?"

"I wasn't sure if you were a Druid. Not at first. Then, afterwards, there were other reasons I couldn't tell you."

"Other secrets you mean?"

"Aye."

She sat with her hands folded demurely in her lap, but Frang knew her mind raced ahead with questions. He wouldn't leave her chamber without baring all to her, and for some reason that didn't seem so hard as it had several weeks ago.

"Why did you leave the Glen?"

Frang smiled ruefully. "Ah, the question everyone at this castle wants an answer to." He looked deep into her amber eyes before reaching out and touching her cheek with the back of his fingers.

He let his hand drop and took a deep, steadying breath. "When I was very young, I dabbled in things that should have been left alone. No warnings could stop me. My curiosity got me cursed."

She blinked and her brow furrowed. "Cursed? By whom? Another Druid?"

He laughed. "If only it had been a Druid. Nay, Kenna, it was something much more powerful than a Druid. A Fae cursed me for my meddling in their affairs."

"A Fae," she repeated softly, her head cocked to the side. "They do exist?"

Frang nodded. "Most assuredly they do."

"You've met one?"

"I've met dozens."

She licked her lips. "Amazing."

Frang leaned his elbows on his knees and waited for the rest of the questions. He didn't have long to wait.

"So, what was the curse?"

"I was to serve the Druids and the MacInnes family for a certain number of years. You see, a prophecy had been foretold, and I was needed to make sure the scales weren't tipped in the other direction."

"The same prophecy you spoke of last night that included Glenna?"

He nodded. "And her two sisters."

"I suppose that since you have left the Glen that the prophecy has already taken place?"

"Aye. The curse ended with the end of the prophecy."

She stared at him, as if reading his soul. "Your leaving was part of the curse, wasn't it? You were made to leave?"

"I was," he admitted. "It was the hardest thing I've ever done. Except coming back."

She rose to her knees and touched his cheek with her hand. "I'm sorry, Frang. If it hadn't been for me, you wouldn't have had to return."

He placed his hand over hers and smiled. "Sacrifices are a part of life, Kenna."

"What did you sacrifice for the curse?" she asked as she gently pulled her hand from his.

Frang briefly closed his eyes. "Three hundred years of my life."

"By the saints," she whispered. "That's why Glenna didn't recognize you? You weren't as you are now?"

She was nothing if not intuitive. "Aye. I was made to look like an old man with a long white hair and a beard that traveled nearly to my stomach."

She giggled and slapped a hand over her mouth. "I'm sorry," she said. "I shouldn't laugh. 'Tis just that I cannot see you that way."

"It wasn't a pretty sight." He joined in her laughter and pulled her up beside him on the chest. "What else do you want to know?"

"How much do you know about me and my involvement with the Wallace?"

Frang blew out a breath and turned forward. "I know that the herbs you gathered for him weren't for his soldiers, but for him alone. He was searching for immortality."

"That night at the castle. Why were you really there?" she asked.

"I wanted to have a look around for myself. To see if my suspicions regarding the Wallace were true."

"And your suspicions about me as well?"

Frang glanced at her and nodded. "I didn't want to believe that you were willingly helping him, but you evaded all my questions."

She nodded. "Making me look guilty. Go on," she urged.

"It was when I searched the castle that I found Wallace's tower. I saw your basket and knew you had been at the castle. It's also when I found the book you carry."

"The Book of Magic. I had no idea that the Wallace had it in his possession," she said as she rose and paced in front of him. "At first, when he asked me for the herbs, I didn't think twice about asking him what they were for. Yet, week after week, he requested I bring him a basketful." She stopped and looked at Frang. "And that's when I began to wonder."

"Did you question him?"

"I tried," she answered. "I didn't want him to think I knew too much, so I couldn't come out and ask him. Yet, no matter what question I put to him, he always had a response that was believable."

Frang nodded in understanding. "Making you want to believe him."

"Aye," she said and crossed her arms over her chest. "He was my laird and had served the clan well. I never thought he could reach for something as powerful as immortality."

"But with the book, he could do much more than that."

"Oh, aye," she admitted solemnly. "He bade me stay at the castle that last night, but I couldn't sleep. I knew he had taken my herbs to his tower, and I wanted to get them back. So, I went there and found not only my basket but the book as well." She dropped her arms and sat beside Frang. "Brigit described the book to me in detail, and she talked about how kings had killed for it. But then it had disappeared for hundreds of years until people forgot about it and it passed into myth."

"A myth it is not," Frang said with a sigh. "You must have gone to the tower after I did. I raced back to your cottage to make sure you were safe as well as to see if you had any involvement with Wallace. Then, I was going to return and take the book."

Kenna smiled. "I beat you to it."

"Aye, you did."

Her smile dropped. "It feels so good to tell you my secrets. They've been a heavy burden to carry."

Frang wanted to wrap an arm around her and pull her against him. Instead, he clasped his hands together. "Kenna, that book is dangerous. Brigit didn't lie when she said men had killed over it. The Wallace won't rest until he has it back in his possession."

"Which is why you stayed?"

He turned to face her and looked into her eyes. "I cannot leave when there is such danger."

"And once the danger is gone?"

He couldn't stop from touching her this time. His hand rose up and pushed a lock of damp hair behind her ear. "I gave my word that I would never return."

20

Frang hid behind one of the ancient stones and watched Kenna with the Druids. She had let her hair hang feely about her, and next to the cream gown, it looked as if it were on fire.

"She's very beautiful."

He looked down to find Glenna standing beside him. "Aye. She is. She fits nicely with the others."

"Any Druid would. How did you find her?"

Frang smiled as he recalled that fateful day. "By accident, I assure you. I was wandering from town to town when I happened upon her, and three men set about doing her harm."

"You saved her?" Glenna asked with a knowing look in her golden-brown eyes.

"I saved her. She was alone and in need of help around her cottage, so I offered to stay and give my aid."

Glenna walked until she stood in front of him then waited until he looked at her. "Why were you going to just leave her last eve?"

"Because I had to. I gave my word, Glenna. The Fae don't take kindly to my going back on a vow."

"Yet you did."

"Aimery knows I had to return. That vow will be forgiven because I had no other choice."

Glenna rolled her eyes. "If they can forgive that vow, they can forgive others. You belong here, Frang."

He didn't argue with her, not when, in his heart, he agreed so adamantly. Instead, he raised his gaze until he found Kenna again. When she turned and her gaze came to rest on him, he found that he wanted to go to her, to discover what all she had learned.

"'Tis strange how things work, isn't it?" Glenna asked as she began to walk away.

"What do you mean?"

"For three hundred years you anchored the Druids here, yet now you are afloat and in need of anchoring. Who do you think will be your anchor, Frang?"

He watched her leave, her words making him consider things he had no business thinking of. He shook his head and searched for Kenna. He found her alone by the stream that ran through the circle of stones, and before he thought twice about it, he found himself walking toward her.

"Want to go for a walk?" he offered.

Kenna smiled and nodded. "Where are you taking me?"

"Somewhere that might interest you. We stopped there last night for a brief time."

She looked interested as she followed him out of the stones and into the forest. "'Tis strange that this forest is so different from mine."

"Not strange, really. This forest may have similar trees, but it holds something yours did not. Druids and magic. That's the difference you sense."

She clasped her hands behind her back as she considered his words. "I think you might be right. In all your travels across Scotland, did you find other Druids?"

"I found hints of them, traces of magic that was old and disappearing like the clouds. The Druids here are the largest concentration of them in Scotland. There are smaller groups, but they stay hidden for fear of what men will do to them if found."

"They have every right to fear men," she said, her mouth pressed in a grim line.

"The Druids live in fear, and because of that fear, our magic will slowly die out. Over the last three hundred years, I've seen the number of Druids dwindle with each passing year. I fear that in another hundred years we will be completely gone."

She stepped around a clump of ferns growing next to a tree. "That is a sad thought. A very sad thought, indeed."

"If I had not spoken of the Druids or had reason to bring you here, you would have married and never said a word to your children of Druids."

Kenna chuckled. "If I had married, you are most likely correct. Men can be small-minded creatures at times. It is unlikely that a man in a clan that knows nothing of Druids as the MacInnes clan does would have allowed me to even speak the word Druid."

"Exactly," Frang said and took her hand to lead her into the nemeton.

She gasped and looked around the small clearing. "What is this place?"

"It is called a nemeton. 'Tis a sacred clearing and is valued greatly by the Druids. Think of it as a fortress of nature separated from the rest of the world."

Kenna laughed as she spread her arms and twirled around in the clearing. "It's so beautiful. The grass is greener, the flowers more bountiful and the colors more vibrant." She stopped and let her eyes roam over every inch of the clearing. "There are more birds and animals here as well."

"Aye. They are drawn to the magic that centers here."

"Magic?" she repeated and looked at him. She licked her lips as she gazed into his eyes and wondered if his body pulsed as her did.

"Do you see that mound over there?" he asked and pointed to the bit of raised earth in the center of the clearing.

She glanced to where he pointed. "Aye."

"That is where you can call a Fae."

Her eyes grew round. "What?"

"If you circle it nine times to the right, it will call a Fae to you."

"Why does it look like there have been fires on it?"

Frang walked to the mound. "During Beltane, the sacred fire is kindled on it."

Kenna followed him and bent to touch the earth. She looked over her shoulder and smiled at Frang. "It feels different here," she said as she straightened.

"It's the magic."

She turned and looked at him, no longer ignoring the

yearning in her heart for him. Try as she might, she couldn't turn away from Frang and the attraction he held over her. "Is walking around this mound the only way you can call a Fae?"

Frang hesitated only a heartbeat. "Nay."

A smile split her face. "Can I meet one?"

"You'll most likely get your chance very soon at Beltane."

"Why do you say it with your brow furrowed and your lips pressed tightly together?"

Frang sighed and pressed the bridge of his nose with his thumb and forefinger before looking at her. She was so beautiful, so full of magic that it hurt just to look at her. The more time he spent with her, the harder it was to ignore his desire for her.

"Because of the Book of Magic. The Fae know you have it. The Wallace knows you have it. Your laird will do whatever he can to get it back, and the Fae will make sure that doesn't happen."

"Then I will give the book to the Fae."

Frang shook his head. "The Fae don't want it either. They cannot touch it."

"Why?"

"I'm not sure exactly. I only know they want no part of it."

Kenna threw up her hands in disgust. "Then what am I to do with it?"

"Destroy it." He swallowed a groan as she took a deep breath, molding her gown to her breasts.

She blinked then took a step back. "Why? It holds such history."

"And spells that men should never see."

Her worried amber eyes peered up at him as she walked toward him. "Did I do the right thing in taking it?"

"Aye. If you hadn't, I would have."

Her eyes glanced away. "You're afraid I'll use it."

It wasn't a question. Frang inhaled deeply. "Curiosity is a trait that all humans have. It's inevitable that someone will open the book to see what's inside it. I fear what will happen once the book has been opened."

"Frang," Conall called as he stepped into the nemeton. "I've been looking for you. I've been sent a missive from the Wallace."

Frang glanced at Kenna before he faced Conall. "What does it say?"

"I think you and Kenna need to return to the castle with me."

To Frang's surprise, Kenna moved closer to him and took his hand in her own. He moved his head to peer down at her and saw her worrying her bottom lip with her teeth.

"It's not a good sign, is it?" she whispered.

Frang squeezed her hand. "I protected you once. I'll do so again."

She tilted her face to him and tried to smile. "I don't know what I'd do without you."

The walk back to the castle was done in silence. Frang didn't release Kenna's hand until they reached the bailey, and only then reluctantly. He had enjoyed having her close to him, and he knew she needed his strength.

Once they were seated in the solar where Glenna awaited them, Conall closed the door and leaned against it. His silver gaze turned to Kenna.

"What was your relationship with the Wallace?"

Frang crossed his arms over his chest and frowned. He had told Conall everything the night before, so he didn't understand why Conall questioned Kenna now.

Kenna glanced at Frang before she turned to Conall. "He was my laird, and I was the clan's healer."

"In the missive I've been sent it states that you were his betrothed."

"Never." Kenna's voice shook with anger, her hands balled into fists atop her lap. "He spoke of me becoming his wife my last night with my clan, but I never agreed."

Frang stretched his legs out in front of him as he studied Conall. "You say you just received the missive?"

"Aye," Conall answered.

"It hasn't even been a day. I would have thought we had a week at least before we heard from Wallace."

Conall nodded wearily. "I did as well."

"He's already returned to his clan," Glenna said as she stared out the window.

"Impossible," Conall stated.

Glenna turned to her husband and chuckled. "What did I tell you about using that word?"

"She right," Frang said. "The Wallace and his men were at least a day behind Kenna and me, yet they managed to nearly catch us."

"Magic," Glenna confirmed.

"He's just a man," Kenna argued. "He's not a Druid, nor does he know the first thing about using magic."

"Maybe not," Frang said quietly. "But he had the Book of Magic. He could have memorized certain spells."

"St. Myrtle's knuckles," Conall cursed under his breath.

Glenna rose and walked to her husband. "I agree, my love."

"What does he want?" Frang asked.

Conall's gaze lifted to him. "He asked for three things. The book, Kenna, and your dead body. In that order."

Frang leaned back in the chair and thought over Conall's words. "In order for you to comply he would have had to issue a threat. What was it?"

"Total destruction of my clan."

Frang heard Kenna gasp and felt a jolt all the way to his toes. He stood slowly. "We'll need to gather the Druids and prepare them."

"You'll need to prepare them," Glenna corrected him. "You are our high priest, Frang. Reclaim what has always been yours."

Frang stared at her a moment wondering if he was strong enough to leave the Glen a second time. Yet, after all the generations of MacInneses had done for the Druids, he couldn't turn his back on Conall now.

"I will see them readied."

Glenna nodded.

Conall wrapped his arm around Glenna and pulled her against him. "The Wallace gave us two days to comply with his wishes."

"He couldn't have returned to his clan," Frang said. "He's been very careful about keeping his search for immortality a secret. I don't think he would allow his men to realize that magic is being used."

Kenna cocked her head to her side. "Do you think they didn't realize how quickly they gained on us?"

"Nay," he replied. "Their focus was on capturing you and nothing else."

She smiled. "Aye."

"What?" Conall asked.

Frang turned him and smiled. "There is no way the Wallace returned to his clan for more men. He's out there. Waiting."

"And if you're wrong?"

"We've got the Druids and Glenna."

21

Kenna sat in the stone circle and tried to find the calm that had left her as soon as she heard the Wallace was going to attack her new home.

Home. Without a doubt, this was her new home, and though she missed her small cottage, she felt as though she belonged here.

Her gaze moved around the circle noting the peace and beauty of the land. If Wallace attacked, everything Frang feared would come to pass. The end of the Druids would happen quicker than any of them expected.

The stream gurgling at her feet and the gentle sway of the trees above her helped to find some peace, but she knew she wouldn't truly find it until the Wallace was dead and the book destroyed.

Yet, every time she thought of destroying the book, she found she didn't want to. What if she needed one of those spells someday to save someone she knew? What if she needed one of those spells to end a great evil? What if she needed one of them for Frang?

Nay, she couldn't destroy it.

Malina, a young, beautiful Druid with light brown hair and smiling hazel eyes sat beside her. "You've been sitting here awhile."

Kenna returned her smile easily. "I've been thinking about how stunning it is here."

"I don't think there's a more beautiful place in Scotland."

"Were you born here?"

Malina nodded. "My mother was a Druid who had traveled from near the border with England, and my father was a member of the MacInnes clan."

"You always knew you were a Druid, then?"

"You could say that," she said with a small laugh. "My two brothers and youngest sister didn't inherit the gifts of being a Druid, though."

"Out of four of you, only you?"

Malina nodded. "That is what happens when one of the parents isn't a Druid, and a chance we all take."

"Have you married?"

"Not yet." But by the way Malina smiled she had found someone.

Kenna sighed wistfully. "In my clan, I was the healer and always alone. I had resigned myself to living out my days by myself."

"You have Frang now."

Malina's words jerked her head around. Frang wasn't hers, nor would he ever be hers no matter how much she wished it so. "Frang is my friend, someone who protected me when others wouldn't. He isn't more than that."

Malina just smiled and rose to her feet. "Only time will tell, Kenna."

For a long while after Malina left, Kenna thought over her words. It was well after midday before she stood and found the Druids gathered together as Frang spoke to them.

"Aye, it is me," he answered someone. "Do not ask how it is so, for I cannot answer you. Conall and the MacInnes clan are in need of us again. Another evil has followed me here and wishes to do us harm."

"Is it Kenna the evil seeks?" a man yelled out.

She saw Frang sigh before he nodded. "It is. The man after both Kenna and me is the laird of the Wallace clan. He is not just a man, though. He is a man who knows some magic, so we must be prepared. Under no circumstances should any Druid venture off MacInnes lands. The magic that keeps us secret is centered in these stones and extends to the boundaries of Conall's land, but they are weakest at the boundaries. If you must leave the stones, only venture as far as the castle. Any farther and I fear what might happen."

"What kind of magic does Wallace have?" a woman asked.

"I don't know the answer," Frang said. "I imagine we'll find out very soon."

Voices rose as questions poured out, but Frang merely held up his hand for silence. Once the Druids had quieted, he continued.

"We have an obligation to keep any Druid safe. Kenna is one of us. The MacInnes clan has kept us secret for centuries. We cannot let anything happen to them. The

Wallace has no idea we are here. We have the element of surprise. And I intend to use it."

Cheers rose up and a relieved smile pulled at Frang's lips. Kenna watched in amazement. Now she knew what Glenna meant when she said this was where he rightfully belonged. He was the leader of the Druids. It was in his soul. He would never be whole away from the Glen. And seeing him with the other Druids made his power and magic more palpable, more physical, almost...erotic.

When his gaze turned to her, her blood quickened. His sky-blue eyes were ablaze with emotion that made her body come alive with heat and excitement. Unable to stop herself, she walked toward him through the throng of disbursing Druids until she stood before him.

"You do belong here," she said.

When he held out his hand for her, she eagerly took it, never questioning him when he walked out of the circle and into the forest.

Each step brought them more solitude, and each step made her more aware of him as a man. They were deep in the forest surrounded by ferns and giant pines when Frang stopped and faced her. His eyes glowed with a strange emotion that made her blood pound in her ears.

"Kenna," he whispered just before his hands cupped her face and his lips met hers.

She whimpered as she melted against him. His tongue licked her lips before it swept into her mouth to dance with hers, sending her spiraling into an abyss of pleasure.

His arms moved until they wrapped around her back and molded her to the hard planes of his body. Kenna's hands roamed over his muscular back to his trim waist while his mouth teased hers with untold delight.

Just as suddenly as the kiss started, it ended. Kenna's body was on fire. Her breasts ached and there was a growing desire between her legs. She stepped away from Frang and turned her back to him.

"Why do you keep kissing me?" she managed to ask him though her voice shook.

"I can't seem to help myself."

"You were going to leave me without so much as a farewell, but you can't stop kissing me?"

She felt him move as he walked up behind her. "I don't understand it any more than you. I'd like nothing more than to lay you down and make love to you." He turned her around until she looked at him. "But you deserve so much more than I could ever offer you, Kenna. You are destined for great things."

"And making love to me would compromise that?"

"Nay. It would be my leaving afterward that would do it."

She frowned. "I thought...you belong here. Everyone knows you've returned."

"I will tell you what I haven't even told Glenna and Conall. I will stay until the Wallace is defeated. And then I will leave, for I have no other choice."

"Even if everyone wants you to stay?"

His finger ran down the side of her face in a soft caress. "Even then."

Kenna didn't want to talk anymore. She only wanted to feel. With a step toward him, she laid her head on his chest and wrapped her arms around him. Instantly, he embraced her, enfolding her in his warmth and magic, his power and safety. She knew as long as she was with Frang, she was safe—except for her heart.

* * *

The Wallace drummed his fingers on his knee as he stared out over MacInnes land. His missive would have been delivered to their laird by now, and he expected an immediate answer.

Out of the corner of his eye, Wallace spotted Callum walked to him.

"It was delivered?" Wallace asked his first in command.

"Aye, laird."

Wallace stood and glared at his man. "Well? Was there an answer?"

Callum visibly swallowed. "He refused to give me one."

For a moment Wallace couldn't believe his ears. "What?" he bellowed.

"Laird MacInnes read the missive and dismissed me. When I asked for an answer, he told me I wasn't getting one yet."

Wallace seethed. "He's bold, this laird of the MacInnes. He doesn't know who he has tangled with offering sanctuary to Kenna and the man."

"Frang."

"What?" Wallace asked, irritated that Callum would interrupt.

"The man. His name is Frang Malcolm."

"Interesting," Wallace said as he crossed his arms over his chest. "A Malcolm, aye?"

"That's the name he gave a few of the men."

"And his interest in Kenna?"

Callum shrugged. "I didn't even know they knew each other."

"He was at the castle?"

"Aye. The night before Kenna fled."

Wallace sighed as it all came together. "Kenna and this Frang were in league together to steal my..." he trailed off as he realized what he had almost revealed.

"Laird?" Callum asked, confusion marking his voice.

Wallace waved his hand in dismissal. "Nothing. I want word sent immediately to me when the MacInnes answers."

He waited until Callum walked away before he let the smile show. It was too bad he no longer had the Book of Magic, but he had a good memory and had been able to memorize some spells. Maybe it was time he tried a few more out.

22

Ever since that kiss in the forest, Frang had thought of nothing but Kenna. Her taste lingered on his lips and her heat stole into his body. He couldn't get her out of his mind. Everywhere he looked, he saw her. Everywhere he went, she was there.

It should frighten him, but it didn't. He couldn't deny he wanted her, needed her.

"Everything all right?" Conall asked.

Frang nodded and concentrated on the food set before him. The great hall was crowded with people for the evening meal, and it was one of the few times he had sat with Conall on the dais. He hadn't been able to tell Conall no, nor had he wanted to since he knew Kenna would also be there.

He found it difficult to concentrate on his food with Kenna only a few seats from him. Every time she laughed or spoke, he found himself leaning toward her to hear what she had to say. He was fast becoming infatuated with her, and it unnerved him like nothing else could.

In his whole existence, there had never been a woman he couldn't forget or walk away from. As it stood now, it would be nearly impossible to walk away from Kenna. Her innocent, sensual kisses stirred feelings in him he'd thought long dead. And the trust that shown in her amber eyes every time she looked at him made him weak. Long ago he'd given up the idea of a wife and family, yet Kenna made him think there could actually be a future between them.

"Frang?"

He stirred and turned to find Conall watching him keenly. "Something wrong?"

"I've asked you that same question three times. I was hoping you could answer it for me."

Frang looked away from Conall's penetrating silver gaze to his platter of uneaten food. "I'm just thinking."

"Since your gaze hasn't left Kenna, I'm guessing she is the one occupying your thoughts."

Frang cursed silently. "Not her exactly, but how I'm going to keep her safe."

Conall nodded and leaned back in his chair. "Do you still have your powers?"

"The powers I had were because I'm a Druid and had nothing to do with the Fae or my immortality. So, aye, to answer your question, I still have my powers."

"I'm glad to hear it since we're going to need them."

Frang reached for his goblet and drank heavily from the ale. When he lowered the goblet, Conall's gaze caught his.

"Why do I get the feeling you're keeping something from me?" Conall asked.

Frang set aside his goblet and turned to his friend. "I'm

not leaving anything out that would endanger your clan or the Druids."

After a moment Conall nodded, accepting his words. "Kenna seems to be settling in all right."

"She is," Frang agreed. "Her teacher was a healer and spoke of the Druids to Kenna. Still, the woman didn't teach her much of the Druids and focused instead on the herbs and their uses."

"That's valuable information."

"Aye. She'll be a great asset."

As if knowing she was being spoken of, Kenna turned and looked at Frang. Her long, red hair had been pulled away from her face and plaited at her temples. Her smile was infectious and Frang found his lips tilting upwards.

"She's quite stunning."

He blinked and glanced at Conall, the smile leaving as quickly as it had come. "That she is. I've never seen hair that shade before. It's a cross between the deep red of a sunset and the flames of a fire."

Conall studied Frang, curious as to the High Priest's words. "Her eyes are also remarkable," he said to see how Frang would respond.

"Very. They're the color of amber."

Conall looked to Kenna to find the woman in question smiling at Frang. There was definitely something between them, something that could blossom into something more. If Frang allowed it.

He cleared his throat to gain Frang's attention. "What did you do these past years?"

"Wandered Scotland." Frang reluctantly looked away from Kenna and focused on Conall.

"Were you searching for something in particular?"

Frang shook his head, his dark hair brushing his shoulders. "I went wherever my feet took me."

"In all those years you never found a place you could call home?"

He hesitated for a moment before answering. "Nay."

Conall considered him a moment before he gave a slight nod of his head. "Nay, I don't guess you would have, not when your heart and soul are here."

"You've the right of it."

"I hear you've become quite the warrior."

Frang's blue eyes hardened a fraction, as if waiting to hear what Conall would say.

Conall smiled before he reached for his goblet. "What did you do before being cursed by the Fae and serving the Druids?"

Frang watched him as he lifted the goblet and drank. When he set it aside, Frang turned to him. "Why do you want to know?"

"You've been a mystery to everyone. I simply want to know more about the man you were."

"The curse did not change me other than my appearance."

Conall leaned forward so only Frang could hear his words. "The hell it did. You were immortal for three hundred years. That would most certainly change a man."

"Do your abilities to tell whether someone lies or not change you?"

"This isn't about me."

Frang's eyes turned glacial. "Answer me. When you

lost your power, you floundered about, but did it change you?"

Reluctantly, Conall shook his head. "You know it didn't. My power only enhances the man I am."

"So, it was the same with me."

Conall leaned back and sighed. "What were you before being cursed?" he asked again.

"Simply a man," Frang said as he stood. "A man who is a Druid."

Conall watched Frang leave the castle, and he wasn't surprised when a few moments later Kenna followed him. Conall turned to his wife to find her looking at him.

"What did you do?"

He chuckled. "Have some faith in your husband, my love."

"You know I do," she said as she took his hand in her own. "Now, tell me what you did."

He smiled at his wife and played with the ends of her dark braid. "I wanted to know more about Frang. And Kenna. I think there might be something between them."

"Most certainly there is," she agreed. "To what extent I do not know, but I think we will discover very soon."

Conall's gaze moved back to the castle door. A smile pulled at his lips. "In less than a week's time is Beltane. The answers we seek could very well be given to us then."

They exchanged a knowing smile. The fires of Beltane drew all Druids, a pull that would not be ignored. Passion could not be denied, and lives were forever changed.

Frang roamed the forest for hours. He knew sleep would elude him, and he needed to clear his head and think. Conall had brought back memories he didn't wish to dwell on.

What were you before the curse?

Frang leaned a hand against an oak and clenched his teeth. A memory of training with his father to be a warrior flashed in his head. He had been destined to die on the battlefield until the day he heard the Druid's call.

He pushed away from the oak and reached behind him for his sword. In one fluid motion he unsheathed the remarkable weapon. He lifted the end of the blade toward the sky, the moonlight reflecting off the metal and the beautiful Fae knot work.

The air moved behind him, subtle and unthreatening. Aimery. Frang ignored the Fae's presence, as he wanted to be alone. When Aimery refused to leave, Frang pivoted and leveled the sword at the Fae commander's throat.

Aimery lifted a brow. "Running from memories is never a good sign."

Frang lowered the weapon and cursed. "I've blocked you from my thoughts."

"True," Aimery replied. "However, it does not take magic to see that the past is haunting you, my friend. I would have thought by now you would have let it go."

"Let it go?"

"It wasn't your fault."

Frang let his head drop back as he sighed. "If I had been there..."

"Enough."

Frang lifted his head and looked at Aimery. The Fae rarely raised his voice, but there was an edge of hardness about him now. Anger rumbled through Frang, anger he knew he could control but refused to.

"Enough?" he repeated. "You have no right to tell me when to leave my memories alone. You have no control over me anymore."

"If you had been with your father and brother that day, you would be dead as well."

Frang ran a hand down his face. "It was where I should have been."

"Your place has always been with the Druids," Aimery said. "You saw what it did to Conall to ignore his Druid side. Can you imagine what life would have been like for you had you done the same?"

"My family depended on me."

Aimery's hand sliced through the air. "Your father hungered for glory, Frang. He knew he couldn't survive that battle, but he had too much pride to turn back. And yet, he brought your brother with him, knowing they would both die. Why do you mourn such a man?"

"He was my father." Frang leaned back against the oak and briefly closed his eyes. He felt something touch his shoulder and opened his eyes to find Aimery's hand upon him.

"You were destined to lead the Druids. It was even your destiny to be cursed so you could ensure the survival of Glenna and her sisters for the prophecy."

Frang's eyes narrowed, and he straightened. "If that's the case, tell me what my destiny is now."

Aimery's hand dropped, and he took a step back, all the emotion erased from his face. "You did the right thing in bringing Kenna here."

But Frang wasn't fooled. "I don't think this has anything to do with Kenna. This has to do with the Book of Magic, doesn't it?"

"It does."

Frang shook his head in disgust as he sheathed his sword. "All the time I've served the Druids, and even the Fae, has not altered how you think of me."

"Do not make the mistake of thinking you know what is in my mind," Aimery said.

"Then, please enlighten."

Aimery sighed wearily. "Frang, you of all people know that we each have our own paths that we must walk. Even I have a path and decisions to make that could alter how my future lives out."

"True, but no one meddles in your life." Anger made his words harsh and clipped, but Frang didn't care.

"The Fae meddle because we want to ensure your realm continues on."

"Like you meddled in giving Glenna, Fiona, and Moira their powers? Three girls whose parents were slaughtered by a madman after power? You gave the girls their powers, you could have stopped MacNeil then. I could have stopped him had I known."

Aimery clasped his hands behind his back. "Despite what you may think, the Fae do not know everything. We discover prophesies or decisions that will alter the future. We have a responsibility to ensure man doesn't destroy your realm."

"This is the decision you spoke to me about when I first left the Glen?"

"Aye."

Frang laughed, the sound humorless and harsh in the still night air. "I've told Kenna to burn the book. I'll make sure it's done on Beltane."

For long moments Aimery simply stared at him. "Be careful, my friend."

In a blink the Fae was gone leaving Frang to stare at an empty spot with Aimery's words echoing in his mind.

"Just what am I supposed to be careful of?"

23

Kenna had looked everywhere for Frang, but he was nowhere to be found. She had told Glenna before she left the castle that she wanted to stay with the Druids for the night. It had been a hasty decision based on wanting to be near Frang.

It was laughable, really. A castle full of warriors and a laird who could easily defend her, yet she wanted to be with the one man who didn't want her.

Kenna leaned against a stone and looked to the moon. A few more days and it would be full, its light illuminating all. With a sigh, she glanced through the doorway in the stones that led to her chamber.

It was spacious inside and warm considering it was carved out of stone. Even the bed had been carved out of the stone with piles and piles of blankets covering it and a small chest off to the side against a wall. A few pegs stuck out from the wall and a small table, and one chair were across the room.

As inviting as her chamber might be, she didn't want to

go inside. Not when the night was so beautiful and her soul so lonely, too lonely to be in her chamber. She wanted to be next to that magic that reminded her of Frang. The sweet song of the Druids settled her restlessness and the desire that multiplied every time he was near.

Kenna raised her face to the stars to find them winking down at her, promising her magic and untold secrets if she could but reach them. She smiled to herself and looked around her. Most of the Druids had gone inside their chambers, leaving only the Druid Warriors to stand guard.

Glenna had told her of the special men who guarded the Druids. Glenna's sister Moira was married to a Druid Warrior who happened to be half Fae.

Kenna was constantly amazed at the magic and possibilities in the Druid's Glen. Even at MacInnes castle she could almost feel the magic pulsing within the stones of the castle.

She had asked Glenna about the need for the warriors since she thought all Druids had powers, so she was quite startled to learn not all did. Kenna looked at her hands. She had no powers, of that she was sure.

Glenna could control fire, her sisters' water and wind, and even her husband could detect if someone lied to him. She had witnessed other Druids who were able to spark a fire to life with only a few words while others could get animals to obey them with only a look.

Yet, what did she bring to them? Nothing but her knowledge of herbs, knowledge these people already had. Frang had told her anyone who heard the music of the Druids was a Druid, but had he lied? Was she really a Druid? Had she brought possible death and destruction to these wonderful people simply because Brigit had spoken of them?

Kenna moved away from the entrance to her chamber, across the rocks that dotted the stream and toward two stones.

"It is late, my lady," a deep voice said from behind her.

Kenna spun to find one of the Druid Warriors. He wasn't dressed in the long, flowing robes that some of the Druids wore or the simple gown that she and others donned. Instead, he was in soft leather pants, a white tunic, and a leather jerkin. She saw a sword, two daggers and a dirk, but she was sure there were countless other weapons hidden on him.

"I cannot sleep," she said after finally finding her voice.

"It isn't wise for you to leave the stones. Frang has asked that all Druids stay close, especially at night."

She nodded. "I'm only going for a short walk. You are welcome to accompany me," she said, knowing he would refuse.

He inhaled deeply, his arms crossed over his chest. "I'd rather you stayed inside the stones."

"I'll be back shortly," she said and stepped between the stones before he could argue with her.

Kenna waited for him to follow, and when he didn't, she let out a sigh of relief. She wanted to be alone for a few moments. She wasn't fool enough to venture far from the stones where the Wallace might find her.

She walked quietly to the nemeton. As soon as she entered the clearing, a smile pulled at her lips. This was just the place she needed to be. Her feet took her to the center where she sat and leaned back on her hands to look at the sky above her.

Her mind instantly moved to Frang, wondering what he was doing and why he had left the great hall agitated. She had left to find him, to see if he was all right, but it had been a foolish idea. He was a high priest and didn't need someone such as her.

As if her mind conjured him up, Frang stepped out of the forest. The light from the moon illuminated him in all his handsome glory in a bluish light. Kenna caught her breath. He looked magnificent, deadly almost with his penetrating gaze that was riveted on her. His thick hair hung to his shoulders and was mussed as if he had run his hands through it several times.

Her body reacted instantly. A warmth unfurled low in her belly and slowly filled her body. Her skin heated, her heart pounded. When his gaze moved lower, she felt her breasts grow heavy and her nipples harden. She bit her lip to keep from moaning as desire thickened the air.

She straightened and watched as he walked toward her, his steps slow and sure. The closer he came the more she realized he was angry and seeking peace just as she was. He stopped before her and stilled. Kenna licked her lips and tilted her head back to look at him.

"You shouldn't be away from the stones." His voice was soft but had an edge to it.

Kenna swallowed and shrugged. "I'm not far. I needed some time alone. Besides, I love looking at the moon."

When he didn't move or speak, she motioned to the ground beside her. "Care to join me?"

To her surprise, he lowered himself next to her and

raised his knees so he could clasp his arms around them. "The Wallace is crafty, Kenna. He'll try any tactic he knows to get you."

"But getting me won't be worth anything without the book."

"He'll use you to barter for the book. Your life for the book. He knows I won't refuse."

Kenna turned her head to look at him. "Don't ever do that, Frang. My life isn't worth him gaining the book. Ever."

Frang's blue gaze met hers. His eyes shown almost eerily in the blue light of the moon. "I gave you my word that I would keep you safe."

"Oh, Frang," Kenna said and raised her hand to his face before she thought about it. As soon as her hand touched him, she felt the pain and anger within him. "I release you of that vow. And surely Wallace isn't as dim-witted as I think he is to attack a clan full of Druids."

Frang's eyes closed as he moved his cheek within her hand. When his eyes opened, Kenna's breath lodged in her lungs.

"I've never seen another woman hold as much beauty as you," he said as he shifted to face her.

Her hand slowly dropped from his face as she stared into his eyes. Her heart beat frantically in her chest as she silently begged him to kiss her, to make her feel as beautiful as he thought she was.

When he moved to turn away, Kenna's gaze lowered, and despair threatened to overwhelm her. But just as suddenly as he moved away, she heard him growl and turn back to her moments before his arms came around her and pulled her against him.

Her face lifted to his, and she saw the confusion and a hint of fear in his blue depths. “Kiss me,” she urged him. “Make me forget everything but you and this magical world you’ve brought me to.”

It was all the urging he needed. Kenna sighed against him as his mouth claimed hers in a fiery kiss that left her breathless and aching for more.

He was relentless in his taking of her mouth, demanding as much as he gave. Her arms wrapped around his chest as he rolled her to the ground.

The feel of his hard body along hers was intoxicating and she longed to feel more of him. Her hands roamed over the hard planes of his back while his tongue plundered her mouth making her moan and shiver in delight.

When he broke the kiss, Kenna gripped his shoulders ready to kiss him again.

“Kenna,” he softly whispered her name. “I’m not myself tonight. I know I shouldn’t be kissing you, but I cannot stop. Be the sane one between us and leave me.”

She heard the urging in his voice, but she also knew he didn’t truly want to be alone. And she most definitely didn’t want to be without him.

“Nay,” she said as she traced his dark brow with a finger. “I want this. I want you, Frang.”

“You don’t know what you’re saying.” His voice was rough with emotion that brought tears to her eyes.

“I do. Take what I am freely offering you. Take me.”

“Kenna,” he said before taking her mouth once again.

The kiss was one meant to claim, a kiss that bespoke of passion long denied and desire so intense it consumed him.

And the kiss left Kenna weak and wanting...more.

She buried her hands in his hair and let herself go. There was no more holding back, no more worry. Only Frang.

When his mouth left hers and trailed down her jaw to her neck, she sighed as new sensations assaulted her. He licked and kissed down her throat to a sensitive spot behind her ear making chills race across her skin and her body heat.

A moan escaped her lips when his body settled over hers. The delicious weight of him as was heady and thrilling. The feel of air on her legs made her eyes fly open to find him watching her.

Little by little his hand inched up her skirts as his fingers trailed over her bare skin. Her heart pounded, her stomach fluttered, and her body heated. Kenna suddenly wanted to see him bared to her as she had dreamt of him in her sleep.

She stopped his hand and gently pushed him off her before she rose up on her knees and faced him. His eyes watched her intently, questioning what she was doing but never stopping her.

Kenna had never been so forward in all her life, but there was something about being with Frang that changed that, that made her want to take chances and live.

In no time she pulled her gown off, kicked away her shoes and rolled down her stockings until she knelt bared before him. Her heart squeezed in her chest as he rose to his knees and reached for her braid. Gently, he loosened her thick, long hair until it hung freely around her.

"Stunning," he said softly. "I've dreamt of how you

would look with your hair hanging around you and nothing else hiding you from my view."

To hear such words from Frang caused her stomach to quiver. She never considered herself anything more than somewhat pretty. She never thought herself a great beauty, but in Frang's eyes she was.

Her hands reached up and unpinned the brooch holding his plaid. As it fell from his shoulders, he reached out and took hold of it. He stood and laid the plaid on the ground before removing his shirt and boots.

Kenna's lips parted on a sigh as she looked her fill of Frang. He stood straight and tall in the moonlight. Several times she'd seen him without his shirt on, but now was different. Now, magic surrounded them.

She stood, letting her hands caress his neck, wide shoulders, and muscular arms. Her fingers trailed down his rippled stomach to his narrow hips before she slowly walked around him until she stood behind him.

There she leaned against him, pressing her body against his back and feeling his heat. She heard him inhale sharply and smiled. And just as she had the front, she let her hands roam over his sculpted back to his firm buttocks.

When she walked back to face him, the look in his eyes was intense, as if he held his body still by sheer will alone. She placed her hands on his hips and looked into his eyes before she swallowed and let her hands roam lower.

As her fingers closed around his rod, he groaned and closed his eyes, his hands clenched at his side. Kenna looked down at the hardness she held in her hand, amazed at how hot and smooth it was all at once.

"Kenna, please," Frang rasped.

Immediately she released him and stepped back only to have him bring her up against him for a fierce kiss that took her breath away. Only vaguely did she realize he had lifted her to place her on top of his plaid.

When he laid atop her, she moaned at the feel of their skin touching. His hardness pressed against her stomach sending her desire shooting through her with each kiss and touch from him.

This was what she had been wanting, what she had been hungering for since that first time she had seen Frang. He was everything she had ever dreamt of in a man.

And for tonight, he was hers.

24

Frang was dying. It was a joyful death, but he was still dying. Just touching Kenna had been pure torture, but seeing her in all her glory and having her touch him had sent him over the edge.

He wanted to plunge inside her heat and feel her pulse around him as she screamed her pleasure. But he would have to go slow. It was her first time, a gift she freely gave him. It humbled him this trust she had in him.

He rose up on his elbows and cupped her face in his hands. Her fingers traced designs over his skin sending delicious shivers racing through him.

He let one of his hands move down her slender shoulder to her side, pausing at her tiny waist before he moved over the swell of her hip to her leg. Her skin was soft and unblemished. Her breasts were large and full, and her pink nipples called for him to taste them.

Frang shifted down her body until his face was even with her breasts. He leaned on one elbow as he cupped one breast in his hand. Kenna sighed and her eyes closed.

When his mouth closed on her nipple and he began to suckle, she cried out and gripped his shoulders as her back arched off the ground.

His rod throbbed with need, aching to be buried inside her. Her hips moved against him, and it was all he could do not to thrust into her heat.

He concentrated on her breasts, suckling first one nipple then the other while his hands kneaded her breasts, and his fingers brought her nipples to hard little peaks. She was writhing against him, her soft moans turning to gasps while her hips moved against his.

With each taste of her, he wanted more. She responded freely to his touch, eagerly giving all that she had when he asked. And he had just begun.

Frang moved to the side of her and let his hand wander over her stomach and hips to her thigh. Gently, he eased open her legs and cupped her womanhood. She stilled, her breath coming in gasps as she waited for what he would do next. He didn't leave her waiting for long. Softly, he opened her woman's lips and teased her opening. Already she was wet. Hot. Wanting. A smile pulled at his lips as her legs opened wider and her hips rose toward him.

Frang pushed a finger inside of her. She was tight and hot. In and out he moved his finger inside her. Her hand gripped his arm and her back arched as she sought her release. When he withdrew his finger, she cried out in frustration. He found her pearl and slowly, lightly began to move back and forth over it.

Kenna's body responded instantly to the caress. Her soft moans gave way to cries of pleasure as he brought her body closer and closer to peaking.

He bent and took her nipple in his mouth swirling his tongue around the hard peak as her nails dug into his back. He could tell she was close to climaxing by the way her body moved against him.

Frang sat up and cupped her breast. He lightly pinched her nipple as he increased his pressure on her pearl. Kenna gasped as her body stilled. She cried out his name when her orgasm claimed her.

But Frang could wait no longer. Already he ached with a need he had never felt before. He moved over her and between her legs, his rod rubbing the sensitive flesh of her womanhood.

He gazed down at her as her face showed the exquisite pleasure rocking through her. And his control snapped.

His rod found her entrance and he pushed inside her heat. He closed his eyes as the pleasure took hold of him. When her arms came around him, he pushed deeper, feeling her wetness engulf him. She was so tight he thought he might spill his seed right then, yet he managed to hold back.

He moved out of her until only the head of him remained before he pushed deeper. In and out he moved, thrusting deeper each time until he felt her maidenhead.

Frang clenched his jaw and gave a mighty thrust, pushing past her maidenhead and burying himself against her womb. He heard Kenna suck in her breath as the pain seized her, and though he wanted to comfort her, his body wouldn't let him.

He made himself hold still, letting her body accept him. But when she moved her leg against him, he lost control.

He began to move inside her, her tightness surrounding him in her heat and wetness.

Before he knew it, his climax was upon him. He gave a final thrust as his seed spilled from his body. Wave upon wave of pleasure stole over him, giving him the peace, he had long sought.

When he at least came to, he looked down to find Kenna watching him with a soft smile on her face.

"I hurt you."

She shrugged. "It is the way of all women on their first time. I didn't mind so much, not when you had given me such pleasure before the pain."

Frang eased out of her and rolled to the side, bringing her against him. He didn't want their world shattered yet, nor was he ready to return to the stone circle. He wrapped his arm around her as she laid her head upon his chest, her warm breath fanning his chest.

"I've never taken an innocent before," he confessed.

She raised her head and kissed his lips. "Other than the small prick of pain, it was very enjoyable. Even at the end. I didn't know it could feel so good to have you inside me."

Frang closed his eyes. "By the skies, don't say that, Kenna. I'm likely to take you again."

"I'm not adverse to that," she said with a laugh.

He opened his eyes and looked at her. He could in fact spend all night making love to her under the stars, but another world called, duties he could not ignore. And a vow that he couldn't disregard.

His hand rose to push a strand of hair from her face behind her ear. "I'm thankful for the gift you've given me."

"I think it was yours to take from the day you first saved me," she said as she lowered her gaze.

Frang sighed and pulled her down against him. Above them, the stars twinkled in the inky sky and a breeze blew through the trees, cooling their heated bodies.

Though Frang knew he should regret giving in to his passion and taking Kenna, he couldn't find it within him. It had felt right to share his body with her, as if he were finally whole.

Now, he worried if he would find the control to stay away from her.

Wallace chanted the spell he had memorized and focused on Kenna. Of all the women in his clan, she had been the only one who hadn't shown him any interest, though he knew it was just a ploy to get him to notice her. And it had worked.

It hadn't taken him long to realized that she would make the perfect laird's wife. She was respected in his clan and sought after by other clans. Her knowledge of herbs was also a plus considering what he needed them for.

His eyes closed as he continued to chant the spell over and over again until the world faded, and Kenna stood before him. She was in a strange formation of large rocks speaking to a woman wearing long white robes.

Wallace's eyes snapped open, and the vision faded. Druids. He had seen Druids. Many Druids.

A smile pulled at his lips as he turned and made his

way back to his men. He called for Callum. "Go to the castle. I want an answer today."

"Aye, laird. Our men won't arrive for another two days," Callum reminded him.

"I know when the men will be here. If MacInnes won't give you an answer, tell him I know his secret."

"Aye, laird," Callum said as he ran to his horse and rode toward the castle.

Wallace rubbed his hands together. A new plan was forming in his mind, one that would get him Kenna, the book and so much more.

* * *

Kenna had woken with a smile. Her night with Frang would stay with her forever, a memory to be cherished and looked at many, many times.

She sighed, a contentedness she'd never felt before coming over her. She looked around the stone circle at the Druids within. Each Druid had their own task to see to each day.

"Are you ready?"

Kenna turned to find Malina standing beside her. She smiled at the priestess. "For what?"

"Frang has told us how knowledgeable you are with herbs and healing. Our best healer, Moira, left some years ago. There are a few of us who are adequate, but nothing that comes close to what Moira was."

"I'll show you all I know," Kenna agreed. "Moira is Glenna's sister, aye?"

"Aye," Malina said as she started off toward the back of

the stones. "She was one of the most powerful Druids I've ever seen."

"More powerful than her sister?"

Malina laughed. "Nay. Each of the three sisters is powerful in her own right. Frang, I believe, is more powerful than the sisters, though you wouldn't know it to look at him. He keeps many things secret. 'Tis just his way."

Kenna smiled inwardly for she knew one secret, a secret shared just between them. "You said Moira was a healer?"

Malina nodded. "She was blessed with that skill, aye."

Kenna spent the rest of the morning showing and explaining herbs to Malina as she recorded everything. It wasn't until noon that Kenna realized she hadn't seen Frang.

She went to the castle hoping to find him but encountered Glenna in the great hall instead.

"Kenna," she called out a greeting from the dais. "Did you fair well in the circle?"

Kenna smiled. "Most certainly. It is very magical there."

"Aye," Glenna said as she patted the bench next to her. "Come sit with me a moment."

"I was looking for Frang," Kenna spoke as she sat.

Glenna nodded. "He, Conall, and some men rode out to the edge of MacInnes land."

"To search for Wallace?"

"Frang is sure he didn't return to his clan. Conall knows we can withstand an attack, but he likes to be prepared for anything."

Dark fear rose up in Kenna. She stood on shaky legs. "Excuse me," she said as she raced back to the stones and her chamber.

She pulled out her bag she had hidden and looked at the book inside. One book wanted so desperately by a man that he would destroy all in its path.

Would Wallace believe that she had destroyed it? Would he take her word for it?

Her answer was a resounding nay. Yet, she couldn't turn it over to him either, not when what he intended to do had become known.

25

"You seem preoccupied," Conall commented as they rode the perimeter of MacInnes land.

Frang frowned. He was preoccupied. He took a deep breath and shrugged. "Maybe a little."

Conall snorted. "Don't try lying to me," he said with a knowing smile.

Frang groaned inwardly having forgotten Conall's ability to detect a lie. He'd never had a reason to lie to Conall, but then again, he'd never shared a night with a beautiful woman under the stars that he didn't want anyone to know about. It wasn't that he was ashamed of what he and Kenna had done, just the opposite actually. It was that he didn't want anyone to think badly of her.

"Leave it alone," he warned Conall.

The smile dropped from Conall's face. "Is everything all right?"

"It will be. Eventually."

Conall raised a dark brow in question. "Did you have a vision of the outcome?"

"Nay, but I have faith that we'll have the element of surprise with the Druids. The Wallace might have a bit of magic he learned from the book, but it's nothing compared to what we have."

"True enough. So, if isn't the Wallace that worries you, it must be Kenna."

He slid Conall a glance. "I asked you to leave it alone."

But the laird ignored him. "She's a good woman. Glenna likes her and the Druids have welcomed her. Do you know that I've already heard talk that some of the priests have taken an interest in her."

"What?" Frang hadn't meant to bellow the word, but he was so surprised at Conall's words, that anger and jealousy had taken over in a heartbeat.

Conall only smiled. "Ah, just as I thought. You've come to care for her."

"Of course, I have," Frang agreed and tried to keep his voice even. He didn't want anyone to know how deep his feelings for Kenna ran. "It was my duty to see she reached the Glen alive and unharmed."

Conall shook his head. "Not exactly a lie, but not the truth either."

Frang looked between the grey's ears and frowned. Ever since he had left Kenna at the entrance to the circle, she had plagued his thoughts. Memories of their shared passion had haunted his dreams, waking him in such a state of need that he had almost gone to find her.

He glanced at Conall to find the laird watching him expectantly. "I'm responsible for her, Conall. Just as I was responsible for Moira, Glenna, and Fiona."

"Aye, but you didn't care for them as you do Kenna. I

see it in the way you look at her. There's no use denying it, nor should you. Everyone is entitled to some happiness."

He didn't bother to answer. They had just crested a hill when Frang drew up and listened. Conall immediately raised his hand to stop his men.

"What is it?"

Frang looked around him, searching until he spotted the rider coming toward them. "Someone comes. It appears the Wallace has waited as long as he intends."

He heard Conall growl next to him. Frang glanced over his shoulder at the two Druid Warriors who had accompanied them. They took their place just behind and to the side of Conall while Conall's men spread out in a line on either side of him and Frang.

They stayed as they were and waited for the rider to approach. Frang recognized the man as Callum, one greatly feared by Wallace's men.

"He's the Wallace's first in command," Frang whispered.

Callum stopped about twenty paces from Conall, his horse jerking his head in agitation when the bit tore at his mouth.

"You'd find your horses last longer if you treated them better," Conall stated flatly.

Callum snorted derisively. "You have bigger concerns than how I treat my horse."

"Really?" Conall looked bored, but Frang knew he was anything but. "Tell me what my concerns are," Conall said.

"You should be quaking in your boots," Callum stated. "My laird is a great warrior, a man to be feared."

"Strange that a man to be so feared has never been heard of before."

Callum clenched his teeth, his jaw muscle flexing. "Do you have an answer for my laird?"

Frang exchanged a look with Conall before Conall turned back to Callum. "I will not give Kenna to you."

Callum's gaze moved to Frang. "And him?"

"You can try to take him," Conall said. "But I wouldn't suggest it."

Callum looked Frang over. "He doesn't look like much."

Frang smiled. "Looks can be deceiving. Why don't we have a go at it?"

He felt more than saw Conall's surprised glance. The old Frang, the one who had lived at the Glen for three hundred years, would never have said such a thing. But the new Frang, he was looking for a fight.

"Another time," Callum said. "You can be sure of it. The Wallace wants you dead and he wants Kenna returned. He always gets what he wants."

"Not this time," Frang said.

Callum sneered. "My laird bid me tell you, MacInnes, that he knows your secret. If you don't want the rest of Scotland to know of it, you'd best think over what he's requested."

"We don't fear you or Wallace," Frang said through clenched teeth. He hated when anyone threatened Conall or the Druids.

They watched Callum wheel his horse around and ride off. Frang lifted a hand and motioned to the Druid Warriors.

"Good," Conall said. "I want to know where they are hiding."

"My warriors will find Wallace and his men, you can be sure of that," Frang said and followed Conall as they returned to the castle.

They went several paces before Conall spoke. "I'm going to post men all along the border. I want advanced notice of more visitors."

"I agree. I'll also send some of the Warriors out to patrol. The Wallace will use magic as well as diversion to gain entry."

"He wants immortality that desperately, aye?"

Frang nodded. "And Kenna. He's obsessed with her." As soon as the words left his mouth, he wondered if he had become infatuated with Kenna himself.

"Kenna needs to be protected, then. She should stay with you at all times."

Frang's heart skipped a beat. To have Kenna all to himself sounded like heaven. "Nay," he forced himself to say. "Glenna would be a better guard. I will be needed elsewhere, and I don't want Kenna anywhere near Wallace."

"You know Kenna best. Where will she feel safer?"

With me, he wanted to shout. Instead, he said, "She trusts Glenna."

As they neared the castle, Frang let his mind search for Kenna, something he had not allowed himself to do until that moment. When he found her in her chamber in the stones staring at the Book of Magic, he knew real fear.

"Frang?" Conall's voice held a note of worry.

Frang couldn't meet his friend's gaze. "Aye?"

"What is it?"

"Each of us has decisions to make. Some could end the world while others will just hurt someone."

Conall stopped his horse and motioned the others to continue toward the castle. "And yours?"

Frang laughed as he pulled up on the grey's reins. "I think I have several, each more difficult than the last."

"You've spoken with Aimery."

He turned to Conall and nodded. "Last night."

"Did he have any news for us?"

"Nay. The Fae won't interfere in this, Conall. We're on our own."

"We could use their help, though."

Frang patted the grey's neck. "We'll get through it. I won't let anything happen to your clan. I give you my word."

"It means a lot," Conall replied. "Don't try to do everything yourself, though. We're all here to help."

Frang watched as Conall rode to the castle. He turned and looked over his shoulder where his warriors had followed Callum. The Druid in him told him to be patient and bid his time until Wallace made a mistake, but the warrior in him told him to confront Wallace and make him leave at once.

Warrior and Druid were at war with each other. Frang had seen what that internal struggle could do to a person. It had nearly destroyed Conall. Would he allow the same?

If he waited, there could be a chance someone might get hurt, or worse, die. There was also a chance Kenna would be taken, something that stole the breath from his body when he thought about it.

Nay, he needed to do something quickly. Maybe then the decisions he would have to make would vanish, just as he intended to make Wallace.

He nudged the grey toward the castle, his thoughts again on Kenna. She had held the book in her hands, and he knew she had contemplated opening it. He prayed she wouldn't delve into the spells, for once she did, there was no turning back.

But the curiosity to see what was in the pages was there, even for him. It was one of the reasons he hadn't taken it from Kenna once they reached the Glen. He had told himself it was safer for her to keep it, but now he knew that had been a mistake.

Somehow, he'd have to get the book from her without her realizing he knew she had thought of opening it. Without a doubt, he knew getting the book would be more difficult than facing Wallace.

He skirted the castle and rode into the forest. An awareness passed over him, alerting him that eyes were watching him, Fae eyes.

"Don't stare, Aimery. It isn't nice," he said without turning around.

Suddenly a woman stepped from behind a tree. Frang instantly halted the grey and jumped from the horse. "Queen Rufina," he whispered. "I had no idea."

She laughed, the sound warm and inviting. "Think nothing of it, Frang. Aimery has been pestering you, I see."

"Nay. He worries about me."

"That he does," Rufina said and pushed her long, flaxen hair over her shoulder. Her shimmering Fae blue eyes regarded Frang a moment before she spoke. "The air is filled with evil intentions."

Frang took in the ethereal beauty that was the queen of the Fae. Her long white gown accented with silver thread stated her position as queen. "There are always evil intentions with man, as you know."

"True," she said. "Aimery has told us you have the Book of Magic."

"I do."

She smiled, her allure strong. "There are times that I wish Aimery hadn't taught you how to block your thoughts from us."

"So you would know if I had looked inside the book?"

"Aye."

Frang crossed his arms and leaned against a tree. "You can always ask. You know I won't lie."

"Have you looked in the book?"

He shook his head. "Though I will admit to being tempted. I know Aimery fears what I will do if I open the book, but that will never happen."

"Stop," she cautioned, her voice harsh and her face holding a thread of fear. "Don't ever say that word, Frang, for I can guarantee there will come a time you will have to make a choice whether to look in the book or not."

Frang dropped his arms and glanced at the ground. "I've already thought of that, Rufina. I don't plan to sit back as Conall would and wait for Wallace to strike."

"So, you would confront the laird now?"

"Aye," he said and walked to her. "If he leaves now everything you and Aimery fear won't come to pass."

She smiled sadly. "You are powerful, Frang, but are you powerful enough to confront Wallace?"

"He knows a few spells. I'm a Druid."

"Think this through," she warned. "The Wallace has no emotion other than hatred in him, Frang. You love this glen and the people too much, and he could use that against you."

"Not if I face him alone."

Her blue eyes sparkled. "Aye, the high priest has allowed the warrior to come out. I wondered how long it would take you to let them both claim you."

"I've seen too many men battle both sides of themselves and lose."

"You're stronger than that," she said. "You are home, Frang. Let the magic of the stones fill you while you find peace in your soul."

"Is that a warning?"

"Most assuredly. You have served the Druids and Fae well for three hundred years. Use the knowledge you have gained to battle the Wallace."

He leaned a hand against the tree and smiled. "Yet, when you cursed me, I was sure you hated me."

Rufina laughed. "I could never hate you, Frang. You have too much good in you."

"Then why did you curse me? I've had three hundred years to think about it, and looking back, what I did was paltry to what others have done."

The queen's gaze looked away from him. "Everything happens for a reason."

"Now you sound like Theron. The king of the Fae has many such sayings. I would like the truth."

Her gaze returned to him. "You meddled where you shouldn't have and paid the price."

"I watched you and Theron doing magic. I really don't think that was meddling."

She sighed. "Frang, you were needed. We knew you were the right person to lead the Druids. Only you could have kept Glenna, Moira, and Fiona safe. Only you. Yet, the prophecy would take place many years after your death. We had to make sure you were still around."

Frang blew out a breath and raked a hand down his face. "Why didn't you just tell me that?"

"You were too young. You had to gain the knowledge as a Druid and the power to be as great as you are. Be safe, and don't do anything hasty."

Before he could respond, she was gone. For a long time, Frang stood in the forest and thought over Rufina's words. He wasn't sure how he felt about learning they had cursed him because he had been chosen by them and not because he had done something wrong. Part of him felt glad to know the Fae had sought him, yet another part was angered that they let him believe a lie for three hundred years.

He took the grey's reins and turned his thoughts from Rufina and the Fae and instead contemplated what he would do with Wallace.

26

The sun was sinking into the horizon by the time Kenna finished with Malina. Her throat hurt from the constant talking and relating of herbs. And yet, they weren't halfway done. There was so much more Kenna had to tell her.

The only thing she thought about on her way to the caves was finding Frang and having him hold her in his arms. Yet, as she slowly made her way through the caves to the castle, she couldn't shake the feeling she was being watched, and every time she turned around, no one was there.

"Hello," she called out.

There wasn't an answer, not that she had really expected one. She started walking again, her eyes searching every shadow and dark corner she passed.

She now regretted her decision to go to the castle to find Frang. All day she had hoped to see him, but he hadn't returned to the stone circle.

Just as she started to turn and retrace her steps to the

stones, she heard something ahead of her. She was passing a tunnel on her left when she heard it again.

Kenna took a deep breath and looked down the darkened tunnel. Only one of the torches remained lit and it was about fifty paces ahead of her. She reached for the torch at the entrance and lifted it from its cradle before she started down the cave.

Every instinct she had told her to run, but something kept pulling her down the cave. An eerie silence surrounded her. The golden glow of the torch she held only added to the forbidding feel of the cave, as if evil itself waited to surround her at its first chance.

In the few times she had walked through the caves, never once had she felt ill at ease. Until now. She inhaled a shaky breath and went to turn around when she thought she heard her name.

She stopped and listened.

"Kenna," a voice whispered faintly.

A menacing chill raced over her skin turning her blood to ice.

"Kenna."

This time the voice was louder, harsher...nearer. With her knees knocking together and heart about to burst from her chest, she turned to run. Only to find Wallace standing before her.

Kenna screamed. She dropped the torch as she tried to run and tripped on her skirts only to fall to the ground.

The Wallace laughed, but there was no mirth in the sound. "Did I frighten you?" he asked.

"How?" she asked, not understanding how he'd gotten into the caves.

"You would be amazed at what I can do, Kenna," he said. "I've come for you. You did something very naughty and took my book. I want it back."

Kenna tried to swallow past the lump of terror in her throat, her hands gripping the rock wall behind her.

"Bring my book tomorrow at midnight on the east side of the forest. There's a clearing. I'll be waiting."

"Nay," she said, suddenly finding her voice.

He leaned over her, his anger and power radiating from him. "If you don't, you condemn this clan and the precious Druids who hide you to death." He straightened. "I'll be waiting for you."

Kenna gasped as he faded from her sight. She pulled her knees to her chest and wrapped her arms around her legs as she lowered her face and let the tears fall.

* * *

Frang breathed in the magic that pulsed through the ground and kept safe generations of MacInnes' families. From his vantage point atop the cliff, he looked down at MacInnes castle and all its occupants. Behind and below him, the Druids kept to the stones. Two different cultures living as one.

Out of the corner of his eye he spotted something moving off to his left. Upon closer look he saw it was the Druid Warriors he had sent to find where the Wallace and his men were hiding. For the first time all day, Frang smiled.

He turned on his heel to meet the warriors only to find

Glenna running toward him. The smile dropped at the concerned expression on her face.

"Where is Kenna?" she asked as she stopped in front of him.

"I don't know."

"She's not at the castle and she's not in the stones. Malina said Kenna left her half an hour ago to come to the castle."

Frang glanced at the warriors riding hard through the forest. They would have to wait. He had to find Kenna. "I'll look in the caves. Take a couple of Druids and look around the forest."

He rushed past Glenna and headed to the entrance to the caves. He refused to believe that the Wallace had gotten past the guards Conall had posted and taken Kenna. Nor did he want to believe that Kenna might have left on her own.

"Kenna," he yelled as he raced through the caves. Over and over, he called her name, his heart pounding with each breath that left his body.

Fear began to take hold of him the longer he searched and didn't find her. He was running through the main cave that led to the castle bailey when he noticed one of the torches gone from a holder at the entrance to a tunnel.

Frang skidded to a halt and unsheathed his sword. He stared down the darkened cave and spotted a torch halfway down. The torch's light only revealed more shadows and questions as to why the other torches were out.

Everyone knew how frightened Glenna was of the caves, and because of that, the Druids kept the torches lit at all times.

With a thought and a wave of his hand Frang lit the other torches. That's when he saw the one lying on the ground. He rushed down the cave to the torch and picked it up. He glanced down the rest of the cave to where it ended at a rock wall.

"Kenna," he hollered, but there wasn't an answer.

Slowly, he stood and retraced his steps. He placed the torch back in its holder. Only then did he calm down enough to think.

After several deep, calming breaths, he closed his eyes and pulled all his power to him as he thought of Kenna. He was about to give up finding her when he caught a hint of fear. He concentrated harder, picturing Kenna in his mind. And that's when he found her.

She sat in her chamber in the stones staring off into nothing, but there was no denying the fear that ran rampant through her.

Frang's eyes snapped open, and he raced toward Kenna. He berated himself for several kinds of fool for not thinking to search for her with his mind first. But he had been so frightened that it had nearly paralyzed him.

He made himself walk into the stones instead of run. He was halfway to Kenna's chamber when he saw Glenna. After a nod to Glenna that told her he had found Kenna, he took the steps down to Kenna's chamber and stopped at the doorway.

Just as his mind had saw her, she sat on her bed, her hands clasped in her lap and her gaze straight ahead. The underlying trepidation he had felt in her filled the stone chamber.

"You've had everyone worried," he said softly as he walked into the chamber and sat beside her on the bed.

She blinked and turned her head to look at him. "I was tired."

He knew she lied, but he let her. "Tell me what you are thinking of?"

"Nothing," she said faintly. "My voice hurts from relaying the herbs and their uses to Malina."

Unable to stop himself, Frang wrapped an arm around her. She crumpled against him, burying her face in his neck. Frang held her with both arms wishing he could take away the fear within her.

"Tell me what has frightened you so," he urged her.

"I thought I could have a life once I left Wallace."

"You can, and you have begun a new life."

"He's here."

Frang frowned and absently smoothed the hair away from her face. "He's never left, Kenna. He's awaiting more of his men to attack. You've known that."

"Aye."

He sighed. "I swore I wouldn't let anything happen to you." He made her look at him. "And I won't."

"I know," she said with a shaky smile.

Her amber eyes gazed up at him. Whereas normally he could see straight into her soul, she had guarded herself. "Why don't you come with me to the castle? I know Glenna would like to see you."

"I'd rather not tonight. I'm going to drink a Willow wood mixture to help my throat."

Frang rose reluctantly. He could tell she wanted to be

alone, and he wondered if she regretted sharing her body with him. "All right," he said as he walked to the door.

At the doorway he looked back to find that she had curled up on her bed. Before he changed his mind, Frang made himself walk from her chamber.

"Is she all right?" Glenna asked.

"I think so," Frang answered. "Her throat aches from talking all day, so she's going to drink some of her herbs and rest."

Glenna rubbed her arms with her hands. "Frang, she wasn't here the first time I came."

"I know," he said and guided her away from Kenna's doorway. All around them Druids worked to prepare for the Beltane festival the next night.

"Something isn't right. She's not right," he said. "I think she was in the caves, but she returned here."

Glenna shivered. "You know how I feel about those caves."

"Aye. We'll have to be careful tomorrow night. I have a feeling Wallace will attack then."

Glenna's eyes snapped fire. "I'll be ready for him."

"Tell Conall. I have some preparations of mine own. I'll see him tomorrow morning at dawn."

He waited until Glenna had left before he silently walked out of the stone circle and into the forest where his Druid Warriors waited.

"Did you find him?"

"Aye," the tallest one answered. Brock was his name. "He is on the east side of the forest near the MacInnes border. He and his men do not hide well, so you should be able to find him."

"Good," Frang said. "How many men are with him?"

Sampson stepped forward. "Twenty, but we heard talk that more would arrive by tomorrow afternoon."

"He's using more magic," Frang murmured. "Did you hear how many would arrive?"

"Nay," Brock answered. "The laird, Wallace, is most always by himself facing toward MacInnes castle. We could have easily killed him."

"I want that privilege," Frang told them. "We cannot allow them to attack. Though they speak of attacking and everything points to tomorrow, I can't help thinking he'll do something before then."

"If he hasn't already," Sampson suggested.

Frang pinched the bridge of his nose with his thumb and forefinger. "Shite. That's a definite possibility. Conall's men are high in the trees as lookouts, but I need as many Druid Warriors as we can spare at the border."

"How much magic does he have?" Brock asked.

"I'm not sure. It may be nothing, or it may be more than we've anticipated. I don't want to chance him using anything on the clan or the Druids. I've worked too long to keep everyone safe for it to be destroyed now."

He looked at the two Druid Warriors, both trained by Dartayous, the greatest Druid Warrior ever.

"Conall will never forgive you if you go in without him," Sampson said.

Frang nodded. "He'll have to get over it. I can't take any chances."

"How many of us do you need?" Brock asked.

"None. I'm going at this alone." He held up a hand

when Brock would have interrupted. "I'm not without powers."

"We know that," Sampson said. "But you are the high priest."

"Was," Frang corrected them.

Brock shook his head. "You still are. Think what will happen if the Wallace captures you."

"Or kills you," Sampson added.

Frang sighed. He would rather do his deed alone, but the warriors had a point. "All right. We leave at midnight."

Wallace rubbed his hands together in glee. It had been so very easy to corner Kenna. He'd had a moment of panic that the spell wouldn't work, but it had. Kenna had believed it was really him standing in front of her.

He laughed. All his life he'd heard whispers of how powerful the Druids were, but from what he'd seen so far, he had more power in his little finger than their entire group.

Aye, taking Kenna and the book was going to be so very easy. And once he had Kenna, killing Frang would take little effort.

He searched his memory for a spell that he had thought he might never use, a spell that was powerful and a little frightening. Now, it appeared, he would have the chance.

27

Frang met Brock and Sampson at midnight and followed them to the Wallace and his men. They went on foot instead of using horses, though it would have been quicker. But Frang wanted secrecy from everyone.

Once they arrived at the camp, he saw how easy it would be for them to kill everyone. There were no guards keeping watch and Wallace was detached from the group.

Just as Brock stepped forward, Frang reached out and stopped him. He looked at the Warrior. "It's too easy."

"What?" Sampson asked. "They're lazy and overconfident."

Frang sat back and studied the camp. "Nay. He's using more magic."

"How can we be sure?"

Frang looked around and motioned to a rabbit that was nearing their camp. "Watch him."

They watched as the rabbit wandered about, but every time it came close to a group of trees, it hastily turned around.

"Shite," Sampson murmured.

Brock's gaze narrowed at the camp. "Then we cannot reach them."

Frang shook his head. "There has to be a way in. I cannot be this close and unable to do something."

Brock rubbed his chin thoughtfully. "Where is he getting his magic?"

Frang hated to lie to him, but the fewer people who knew about the book the better. "I don't know."

"If he's protecting their camp, he's more powerful than I thought," Sampson said ruefully.

Frang motioned for them to leave. Once they were a safe distance away, he turned to the men. "We'll have to return tomorrow night. Maybe when his new men arrive, he'll let down whatever magic is protecting them."

"Then we attack," Sampson said with a smile.

Frang nodded. "Then we attack."

"Tomorrow night is Beltane," Brock reminded them. "You've duties."

"Aye," Frang said. "I'll do my duties and be finished before midnight. Everyone else will be occupied, so we'll be able to sneak off."

"Until then," the Warriors said before drifting off into the night.

Frang quietly made his way back to watch the camp. The Wallace had to have a weakness. And Frang intended to discover what it was.

* * *

It was well past midnight when Kenna rose and stroked her fire to life. Once she bolted her door to make sure she wouldn't be disturbed, she pulled out the Book of Magic.

For a moment, she simply stared at the beautiful book. Her finger traced the knot work along the edges. The black stone with a red center in the middle of the book was cool to the touch, as if it waited to come alive.

She reached to open the book but hesitated. She bit her lower lip as she thought over what Brigit had told her of the book. It was very powerful and had spells that could alter the course of time. Or so Brigit had said.

But Brigit had also said that every time someone used a spell a piece of their soul died. It was addictive she had warned. So addictive men had murdered for the book, and even killed their own families to procure it.

Kenna liked to think she was stronger than that, but probably most who had read from the book had that same thought.

Frang's image formed in her mind. He had been so gentle and loving with her when he'd take her innocence. She hadn't missed the look of pure bliss in his eyes when he had emptied his seed inside of her.

She thought of the Druids and Conall and his clan. All needed protection from Wallace for she knew without a doubt he would stop at nothing to destroy them if she didn't give herself and the book over to him at midnight tomorrow.

Beltane.

It was to be her first as a Druid, and she had looked forward to seeing the celebration as well as participating. Malina had told her that she would see a Fae.

But it might be too late by then. The Wallace threatened death to everyone if she didn't show tomorrow night. But what if she did go to him? What if she went without the book but with a spell that could stop him?

A smile pulled at Kenna's lips. It was her only choice. She knew if she went with the Wallace, Frang would come after her, and it was just what Wallace wanted. The thought of Frang injured or dead left her sick to her stomach. He meant too much to her for her to allow something to happen to him.

Besides, the Druids needed him as their high priest. He had made a vow to her to protect her, but she couldn't allow him to keep that vow. If she failed to kill the Wallace as she planned, she needed to make sure Frang would never come after her.

With a deep breath, Kenna opened the book. In big, bold letters the first page read:

The Book of Magic

Read at your own peril

Kenna shivered and flipped to the next page, which featured a Summoning Spell. Page after page she read seeking the spell that would answer all her prayers.

The sun was cresting the horizon when she finally found what she wanted. Over and over, she read the spell, memorizing every line until she could repeat it without forgetting a word.

She closed the book and hid it once again. Only then did she ready herself to face the day and Frang, for she knew he would come to her again. She had lied the night before and he had let her.

How many more lies would he let her speak before he

realized her intent? She prayed that it was well after she had finished her task with the Wallace. Then she would ask his forgiveness for using the book.

She touched the dagger she wore under her skirts. If the spell failed, she'd use the dagger as Frang had taught her. She would not fail. She could not fail.

* * *

By the time Frang returned to the stone circle, the sun had risen. Exhaustion pulled at him, but he refused to give in. Too much was at stake for him to fall asleep now.

He'd planned to take a quick nap for an hour or two this morning when no one would miss him. Preparations were already underway for the great celebration. Already a sensual feel had overtaken the Glen. It was always so on Beltane, and Frang had joined in the coupling through the years as did nearly every Druid.

Just thinking of being with Kenna again left him aching and hard. One taste of her hadn't been enough. He wanted, nay needed, her again.

With his mind so preoccupied he was more than surprised to find Conall in his chamber. Frang paused at the doorway before shutting the door and continuing into the spacious chamber carved out of the rocks.

His large bed stood against the far wall covered in green and black material. He glanced at Conall who sat on the bench at the foot of the bed, his elbows on his knees.

"What brings you here, Conall?" Frang asked as he walked to a small table near the right corner that held a bowl and a pitcher of water. He poured the water in the bowl and splashed it on his face.

Few people ever came inside his chambers, and the fact that Conall hadn't waited for him to enter told Frang Conall might very well know what he had planned.

"You know what brings me here," the laird said softly.

Frang dried his face and turned to face Conall. The soft tone bespoke anger. Frang leaned his hip against the table and crossed his arms over his chest.

"I'm afraid I don't."

Conall straightened. "You've been gone all night."

"Since when do I answer to you?"

"You don't, damn you." Conall stood and raked a hand through his hair as he turned his back to Frang.

For several moments Frang watched his friend. Finally, he lowered his arms and moved to the bed. "I cannot help you if I don't know what bothers you."

Conall turned back to Frang. "You might have changed since your return, but there is one thing that has never altered about you, you never go back on your word."

"Nay."

"You must fear Wallace greatly to plan on attacking him yourself."

Frang blinked, unable to believe Conall knew his plans. "What makes you think I'd do something so daft?"

"It's what I'd do."

Frang sighed. "It would have been better had you thought otherwise."

"Why? So you could get killed?"

Frang sank onto his bed and leaned back against the headboard. "He's powerful, Conall. Very powerful. I went to his camp last night to attack, but he has a shield of some kind up where nothing can get in."

Conall's jaw slackened. "He cannot be more powerful than you."

"I don't know," Frang admitted. "I haven't tested my powers against him, and I didn't want to. I'd rather have killed him last night to save everyone the trouble of an attack."

"What's your plan now?"

"He has more men arriving this afternoon. I stayed near his camp all night trying to find his weakness."

Conall brightened. "Did you?"

"It appears he has two."

"That's better for us," Conall said with a smile. "We'll use the weaknesses against him. What are they?"

"Kenna and the Book of Magic."

The smile dropped from Conall's face. "Shite."

"Exactly," Frang said and dropped his head back to rest on the headboard. "Nothing was said, but I have a feeling he'll attack tonight."

"Tonight? Why?"

Frang raised his head. "He knows there are Druids here."

Conall blew out a breath and leaned against the wall. "Our best defense is to attack him first, before his men arrive."

"You'll never get through his shield."

"And if we draw him out?"

Frang shook his head. "He won't fall for it."

"What if we use Kenna as bait?"

He clenched his jaw. "Nay. I don't want her near him."

Conall stared at him a moment before he shrugged. "It may be our only chance."

"Between Glenna and I we should be able to handle Wallace."

"Maybe I should have sent for Fiona and Moira. The three sisters' combined magic is a powerful thing."

Frang chuckled. "That it is, but there isn't time for them to get here."

"Do you have a plan then?"

"I do."

Conall leaned a shoulder against the wall. "And I suppose this plan doesn't involve Kenna?"

"Do you remember when MacNeil came here for Glenna? Do you remember the fear you felt when you thought your wife might be taken from you?"

"I will never forget that, aye."

"Then you'll understand why I need to keep Kenna safe. I gave my vow to her that the Wallace would never harm her again. I cannot go back on that vow. I won't go back on that vow."

Conall nodded. "I trust you, Frang. So, what is the plan?"

Frang smiled and leaned forward as he began to explain his intricate strategy.

28

The day went by too fast for Kenna. She had been with the other Druids getting ready for the great celebration of Beltane, which occupied her entire day. The joyfulness that ran through the land of MacInnes was only overshadowed by the sensual vibration that seemed to surround everyone. Kenna had heard of Beltane from Brigit, and she was anxious to experience it firsthand.

Her gaze moved to the sky to find the sun well past its zenith. She took a deep breath and went over the spell again in her head. Every time she thought of facing Wallace, her palms began to sweat and her stomach fell to her feet.

"Come, Kenna," Malina called as she raced toward the loch.

Kenna picked up her skirts and raced after her new friend, Malina. "What are you doing?"

"Preparing for tonight," she said as she took Kenna's hand and pulled her faster down the rocky slope of the hill to the loch.

Kenna lost her footing and slipped, but with the help of Malina managed to catch herself.

"Careful," Malina said. "You wouldn't want to be injured for tonight."

"What exactly happens?" Kenna asked.

Malina smiled wistfully as she reached the edge of the loch and began to disrobe. "It's beautiful and magical, Kenna. The veil between our world and the Realm of the Fae is so thin that the Fae cross over. The magical fire is lit and there is much dancing and merrymaking."

"Sounds lovely." Somehow Kenna knew there was more to it, but she didn't ask as she pulled her gown off and tossed it to the ground.

Malina laughed and took her hand as she pulled her into the water. "Come on and I'll prepare you."

"Prepare me?" Kenna echoed as the water surrounded her. She sunk beneath the water and swam a ways before she surfaced. "Now tell me what you mean by preparing?"

Malina leaned back to wet her head, her breasts thrusting upward. She wiped the water from her face as she straightened and sunk into the water until it reached her neck. "If you're lucky, one of the Fae will choose you for the night."

"Choose me for what?"

"To make love to," Malina said with a giggle. "Last Beltane I spent the most glorious night with a Fae. I've never been loved like that before, and I don't think I ever will again."

"Do you think he'll find you again tonight?"

Malina shrugged. "It doesn't matter. You haven't met a Fae yet, so you don't know."

"Don't know what?"

"How sensual they are. Just to look at one makes most women want to take them right there."

Kenna bit her lip at the image Malina's words gave her. "And if you don't want to bed a Fae?"

Malina looked at her as if she'd suddenly grow a fin. "Who wouldn't want a Fae? Besides, it is in their makeup, this sensual side of them. We cannot ignore it. It's one of the reasons you don't see the Fae walking among us."

"I see."

Malina threw a bar of soap at her splashing Kenna in the face. Kenna reached for the soap and began to bathe, her mind on Frang and if he would find a Fae to join with that night.

She didn't like the jealousy that sprang up in her, although she tried to tell herself she didn't have the right. One night did not make him hers.

But you want him.

Oh, aye, she most certainly did want him. Even now her gaze searched for him, hoping to catch a glimpse of his plaid or dark hair and bright blue eyes.

But Kenna and Malina weren't the only ones readying for Beltane. The loch was soon swarming with Druids and clans people alike, each eager for the coming of the night.

Kenna finished rinsing her hair and watched as Malina walked out of the water as if she walked naked all the time. Kenna looked around but found that no one was paying any attention to Malina.

"It's all right," Malina said as she motioned Kenna to follow her.

Kenna moved into shallow water and wrung her hair

dry before she stood up and walked out of the water. She tried not to sprint to her gown, but she didn't walk either. She had just snatched up her gown and held it to her body when a shiver of a gaze raked over her.

Her eyes looked around her before her gaze moved toward the castle. Atop the hill overlooking the loch stood Frang. Staring at her.

She raised her hand in a silent greeting and smiled when he returned her wave. She started to move toward him when Malina took her arm.

"We're not finished," she said and tugged Kenna away.

Kenna glanced back only to find that Frang had disappeared. Reluctantly, she went with Malina, but her thoughts were on Frang and how she could get him alone before a Fae found him.

Frang cursed as he turned on his heel and walked away from the loch. He didn't know what brought him to the loch, but once he'd caught sight of Kenna, he hadn't been able to turn away.

She was easy to spot with her deep red hair that looked like fire in the water. And when she had left the loch to walk naked to her clothes, he had been glad to get a glimpse of her lithe body.

But that glimpse had only made him hunger for her more, if that was possible. It didn't take much at all to remind him of the loving they had shared, the kisses, the caresses, the complete and total surrender on his part.

He frowned and continued to the stones. It was time

for him to ready himself for the celebration. Once inside his chamber, he stared down at the white robes laid across his bed. Ever since he had become high priest, he had worn the white robes. Never once had he considered not wearing them. Until now.

How long he stared down at the garment, he didn't know. So far everyone had accepted that he had returned looking much younger than when he'd left. Few had questioned him, as they all suspected it had something to do with the Fae.

But could he face them all without the robes? And did he want to?

He was still Frang the Druid High Priest, but he wasn't the same man who had lived within the stone circle for three hundred years. The warrior in him had been released, and it didn't want to be put away.

Especially not when Kenna was in such danger.

Conall and the Druid Warriors can easily protect her. Why are you so adamant about doing it?

Frang clenched his jaw as he struggled to answer his own question. Why was he so intent on making sure he was the one to protect Kenna? It wasn't just about his vow, of that much he was sure.

But the real reason? He wasn't even sure he could answer that. Or wanted to for that matter.

As much as he wanted to dwell on his feelings for Kenna, he couldn't. There wasn't time. Already he felt the pull of the nemeton on him. He snatched the white robes from his bed and hurriedly jerked them on over his tartan.

He was both warrior and high priest. He would wear the robes and his tartan. His gaze moved to his sword that rested near the door. Though he longed to wear it in case he needed it, he chose to leave it for the time being. There would be time enough to get it before he went hunting for Wallace.

Frang left his chamber and stood amid the circle of stones. To anyone looking in, the inner circle was barren and empty. Only the ones that truly believed could see through the fi-fiade.

It was magic within the stones brought to life by the Fae that granted the Druids their home and safety. It was magic that gave them the chambers.

He placed a hand on one of the stones that reached high into the sky and closed his eyes as the magic pulsed under his palm. His hand tingled and warmed as the magic pooled and seeped into his body.

When he removed his hand, he opened his eyes and looked at his palm. He could still feel the magic moving inside of him, and he wondered if that was how the Fae felt in their realm where magic existed in everything.

For five years he had lived without the magic that was so evident here. It was going to be very difficult to leave it behind again.

The shadows around him lengthened and caused him to move his gaze to the sky to find the sun all but gone over the horizon.

It was time.

29

Glenna looked out over the land. The call for the Druids to gather in the nementon was strong and she couldn't ignore it much longer.

"Ready, my love?"

She turned to find Conall at the doorway to their chamber, a wicked grin on his handsome face. It had been Beltane five years ago that had made both of them realized the passion between them couldn't be denied. It was a special time for both of them, and each year they celebrated the day to the fullest.

"I am," she answered and walked to him.

When she reached him, he took her hand and stopped her. "What bothers you?"

"Frang. I worry that, despite what he told you, he will do something alone."

Conall led her out of the chamber and down the hallway. "It isn't Frang I worry so much over as Kenna."

"Kenna?" She hadn't given much thought to Kenna doing anything other than hiding. "She's very fearful of the

Wallace. I cannot see her doing anything that might endanger herself."

Conall smiled ruefully. "You forget one important fact, my dear wife. She cares for Frang."

"She does, but enough to risk her own life?"

He shrugged. "I cannot answer that."

Glenna sighed loudly as they walked down the stairs. "Both Frang and Kenna are willing to risk their lives for the other. Do you think they know how deeply their feelings run?"

"Nay," Conall said as he led her out of the castle and into the bailey. "Frang tells me he made a vow to her and that he must protect the Druids, but even I can see that he does it solely for Kenna."

"I hope he doesn't wait too long to realized it," Glenna said as they entered the caves. "You would think after all this time I wouldn't still shiver each time I enter these caves."

Conall chuckled. "I've got my sword and can easily slay any spiders that dare to venture near you."

"Thank the saints for that," she whispered while her gaze darted about looking for any eight-legged creatures that might scurry at her.

By the time they reached the forest, Glenna began to feel sick. She placed her hand over stomach and smiled. She had a secret she would share with Conall this night, a secret she had carried for several weeks now.

She stopped near a tree and rested. Conall was immediately at her side, his face lined with concern.

"Glenna? Are you not feeling well?"

She smiled up into his silver gaze. “I'm just a little tired.”

“You haven't been sleeping well. Have you had more visions you haven't told me of?”

“I tell you everything.” She laughed and tried to move away, but Conall held her.

“You're not moving until you tell me what is wrong. I know you too well, my love, for you to tell me nothing is wrong and expect me to believe it.”

“I'm tired is all,” she lied.

His face set in hard lines as he looked down at her in his most sever expression. “Glenna.”

“You're impossible,” she hissed. “I was going to surprise you later, but since you have to know now, I'm carrying our child.”

His face froze in surprise. “Are you sure?”

“Positive.”

He crushed her to him and swung her around raining kisses on her face.

When he finally set her down the world was still spinning. “I gather you're happy.”

“You know I am,” he said as he leaned down and kissed her. “Thank you.”

“You're welcome, though you did have something to do with it.”

He took her hand laughing. “Come. I want to share this news with everyone.”

* * *

Frang stayed a moment longer after Conall and Glenna had walked off. He was very happy for them, but he also found that he was sad, sad because he had never known until that moment that he wanted to share that kind of joy with someone.

The love that shown in their eyes amazed him each time he saw it. It was the same with Fiona and Gregor as well as Moira and Dartayous.

He began to wonder if he'd ever feel that way about a woman, and no sooner had that thought entered his mind than an imagine of Kenna flashed in his head.

Frang pushed her from his mind and started toward the nemeton. He had just entered the clearing and walked to stand behind the huge pile of wood atop the mound when he felt the air shift around him.

He looked over his shoulder to find Rufina and Theron behind him. He nodded to the king and queen of the Fae before he turned back to the fire. He raised his hands over the wood as the crowed quieted and with just a thought the pile was engulfed in flames.

Through the crackling flames, he spotted a face in the crowd of Druids, a face that haunted him night and day. Kenna. She was breathtaking with her red hair loose and flowing about her shoulders and back. The hair at her temples had been pulled away from her face and held in place by small white flowers.

He watched as she moved through the people, her cream gown being replaced by the simple robes of a Druid priestess. Hers were pale blue, signaling her a healer.

Of their own accord, his feet moved toward her. The need to be near her, to hold her in his arms was overwhelming. Their gazes caught and held as she stopped and faced him.

Something took hold of his arm. Frang pulled free and continued to Kenna. But the hand refused to let go for long and soon returned.

With a growl Frang turned to whoever dared to stop him, his hand on the dagger at his waist, only to find Aimery staring at him with one brow raised.

"Do you plan on using that weapon on me?" the Fae commander asked.

Frang took in a steadying breath and moved his hand away from the dagger. His gaze moved to Theron and Rufina to find them watching him as well.

With a curse Frang realized where he was and what he was supposed to be doing. Aimery hadn't wanted to prevent him from being with Kenna, he was reminding Frang that he had duties as a high priest.

"The night is young. There will be plenty of time for you to find her again," Aimery whispered before he moved back next to his king and queen.

Frang once again took his place in the center behind the fire and faced the Druids and others who had come to rejoice in Beltane.

"Once again we celebrate the return of the sun," he said, his voice rising to be heard over the fire. "This is the night where the veils between our world and the Realm of the Fae are thin, a night when the Fae walk among us."

Rufina and Theron moved on either side of him. Frang's gaze found Kenna's. "We welcome the Fae and the gifts their presence grants us. Celebrate!"

As soon as the last word left his mouth sparks flew from

the fire and Fae began to appear. Most were already nude while others still wore the cloths of their realm, though they didn't stay on for long.

Ecstasy hung thick in the air as couples began to move off together. Yet, Frang's gaze never left Kenna. Her eyes had widened at the appearance of the Fae. Her curiosity was high, and it was apparent she longed to speak to one.

King Theron turned to Frang, demanding his attention. "I've never seen you come clothed in a plaid before."

Frang immediately took offence. "I still wear the robes of my station, but I will not deny that I am also a warrior."

A soft hand touched his arm, and he swiveled his head to Rufina. "It doesn't matter to us what you wear, Frang. Theron was simply curious."

"Forgive me," Frang said and clasped his hands in front of him. He had to get control of himself.

"There is nothing to forgive," Theron said. "I'm glad to see that you've returned."

"Wasn't it your intention to keep me away?" Frang asked. "It was part of the stipulation of the curse?" He glanced at Aimery who watched them intently.

Theron sighed. "Frang..."

"It doesn't matter anymore," Frang interrupted him. "Rufina told me why I was cursed."

"She did?" Aimery asked as he stepped forward. "So, you know everything?"

Frang nodded. "I know I was needed, and instead of telling me, they cursed me. Regardless, the end was the same. I accept that what they did, they did for us."

Aimery smiled. "I've wanted to tell you for a long time."

"Thank you," Frang said. He glanced over to find a Fae speaking to Kenna and all control he had snapped.

Aimery crossed his arms over his chest as he watched Frang stalk toward Kenna and the Fae she spoke with. "Do you think he knows yet?"

Rufina laughed. "You mean does he know he's in love with her? Nay, not yet. But he will," she said.

Theron chuckled. "It is a good night. Glenna just told Conall that he will be a father, and Frang has found love."

"That's wonderful," Rufina said at the news of Glenna. "I know how desperately she has wanted a child."

But Aimery wasn't ready to celebrate. "Kenna still has the Book of Magic."

Rufina's smile faded. "Have faith in Frang, Aimery. He will make the right decision."

"It isn't him I don't have faith in, my queen," he said. "It's everyone else."

Theron's hand came to rest on Aimery's shoulder. "We cannot interfere."

"I know."

"But no one said we couldn't watch."

Aimery smiled. "My king, you are all that is wise."

Rufina harrumphed. "Wise? Why don't you tell him whose idea it was?"

Aimery bent and kissed his queen's hand. "I am ever your servant," he said before he moved into the forest.

Theron took a deep breath and turned to his wife. "Once again, the fate of the Glen hangs in the balance."

"All will be well," she said as she leaned her head against him. "I feel it in my bones."

"I pray you're right, wife."

* * *

Kenna had never seen someone look so powerful or handsome as Frang had as he began the ceremony. He commanded the Druids with just a look, his tone deep and smooth as he called forth the Fae.

Malina had leaned close and explained the man and woman on either side of Frang were the king and queen of the Fae. Before Kenna had time to register that thought, Fae began to fill the area. Their graceful, beautiful bodies bared for all to see.

She stared in wonder as the Fae chose their human companions for the night, sometimes with no words spoken, before they disappeared into the forest.

Kenna was trying to decide whether to approach Frang or not when she felt something about her, as if a cloak of desire had been placed on her.

Kenna.

She looked to her left and saw a magnificent male Fae striding toward her. He was more beautiful than words could describe with his swirling blue eyes, flaxen hair, and tall form. He wasn't as muscular as Frang, but there was strength in him, nonetheless.

Her gaze moved over his nude body to his thick rod that hardened before her eyes. She gasped as he came to stand before her.

Touch me.

She blinked and looked into his eyes. "Stop talking to me in my head."

Why? 'Tis what we do. Stop denying the desire you have for me. Take my hand and I will show you a night you will never forget full of pleasure and rapture.

Kenna looked down to find the Fae's hand outstretched and waiting for her. Her hand lifted as if she no longer had control over her body.

Suddenly, the Fae's gaze moved over her, and Kenna heard someone approach.

"Release her, Daryn."

Kenna looked over her shoulder to find Frang.

"It is me she wants," Daryn said softly.

Frang shook his head. "You're using your allure. Let her make her own decision."

"What is she to you?" Daryn asked, not ready to give up.

Kenna looked back and forth between the two men. She wanted to go to Frang, but her body refused to listen. It was as if the Fae had control of her.

"Kenna," Frang said and gently turned her to him. "Take my hand and come with me."

Her breath left her in a whoosh as Daryn came up behind her and molded his body to hers.

"Aye, Kenna," Daryn whispered in her ear. "Tell him who it is you really want."

The world spun around Kenna as her body began to throb with desire. Daryn's hands caressed her back and sides as he moved his rod against the swells of her bottom.

"Kenna," Frang said and placed his hands on either side of her face. "I've never wanted a woman more than I've wanted you. If you want Daryn, I'll leave. You have only to say the word."

She focused on Frang's beautiful sky-blue eyes and

smiled for she knew what it was she wanted. "You. I want you."

As soon as the words were out of her mouth, Daryn backed away from her and left, yet the desire she felt only increased. All she could think of was having Frang's rod buried deep inside of her again.

"Come," he said and led her out of the clearing and into the forest.

Kenna lifted her skirts with her free hand since she had to nearly run to keep up with his long strides. She heard a familiar laugh and caught sight of Malina disappearing with a man who looked somewhat familiar, but she didn't think twice about her friend, not when she was with Frang once again.

Frang didn't slow until they entered the stone circle. She began to think he was taking her to her chamber when he suddenly turned and opened a door.

She paused and looked at him before entering. She heard the door close softly behind her, but her gaze was taking in the room. Without a doubt she knew Frang had taken her to his chamber.

"I've never brought a woman here," he said as he came up behind her and moved her hair away from her neck before he bent down and placed his mouth against her skin.

Kenna sighed and leaned against him. "Why have you brought me?"

He lifted his head then turned her to face him. "I wish I knew the answer."

"It doesn't matter," she said with a smile. "Kiss me."

As soon as his lips claimed hers, the need that had

pulsed within her exploded. She heard fabric ripping as she and Frang tried to take the other's clothes off.

He broke the kiss only long enough to pull off his boots, dagger and kilt, then his mouth was once more on hers, kissing her mindless. Kenna threw off her robes and let him guide her back toward the bed as her hands roamed over his back, his muscles bunching and moving beneath her palms. Her breasts ached for his touch while her body sought his heat.

He lifted her and gently laid her on the bed before moving on top of her. She smiled up at him as he settled between her legs. He moved his hips against her sex sending waves of pleasure through her.

She moaned and closed her eyes as he repeated the movement then bent down and took a nipple in his mouth. His hand moved to cup her sex, his fingers adding a little pressure to her pearl. Her desire climbed higher, and her body throbbed for release.

"Frang," she whispered as she moved her hips against him.

She heard his sharp intake of breath before he moved down, his mouth trailing kisses to the valley of her breasts, then down her chest and across her hips.

It wasn't until he pushed her legs open wider and his mouth hovered over her sex that she realized what he intended to do. Her breath stuck in her throat as she watched his head lower between her legs. Then, she felt his tongue flick over her.

She gasped and dug her fingers in the covers as intense pleasure wrapped around her. While Frang's tongue swirled around her pearl, his hands found her nipples and teased them mercilessly.

He pinched her nipples before rubbing his thumbs back and forth over them making them hard, sensitive peaks that begged for more of his touch. But it was nothing compared to what his tongue was doing to her sex.

She felt herself building toward her climax with each stroke of his tongue, but just before she peaked, he rose up and kissed her. Kenna wrapped her arms around him as she tasted herself on his tongue.

"My God." Frang leaned his forehead against hers and looked into her eyes. "I cannot get enough of you."

"Good, because I want so much more of you."

He smiled just before he rose up and flipped her on her stomach. As innocent as she was in the ways of lovemaking, she trusted Frang. Instead of being fearful of what he was doing, she found herself curious and eager for his touch. She sighed contentedly when his hands began to roam over her back and buttocks. His caress was light, gentle but bespoke of a promise of pleasure to come.

He didn't leave her long to wait as he licked her from neck to the small of her back. She shivered and waited for more. When he lifted her hips up until she rested on her elbows, excitement began to drum through her.

His hands massaged her bottom as he rubbed his rod in the cleft of her cheeks. Just when she didn't think she could stand it any longer, he slowly entered her. Kenna cried out as he impaled her. She had forgotten how thick he was, but it didn't take her long to stretch to accommodate him.

All the while, he stayed still. When she tried to move her hips, he gripped them and held her.

"Don't move. I'll spill now if you do."

She didn't care. All she wanted was the release she felt so very near, if only he would move within her.

"Frang," she cried, her face buried in the covers.

Gently he pulled out of her only to thrust hard into her. Over and over he moved, her climax growing closer and closer. She was almost to the edge.

"Kenna," she heard Frang call her name.

He was pumping furiously in her, and then she felt him move until his fingers gripped her pearl. Between his thumb and forefinger, he rubbed her tiny bud as he continued to thrust.

As the orgasm washed through her, she heard Frang call her name as his seed filled her body.

30

Frang couldn't breathe, couldn't move. Something had happened. He couldn't name it, couldn't say what it was, but he knew something had changed.

Kenna looked over her shoulder at him and smiled. He leaned down and kissed her before he slowly pulled out of her and fell to the bed. He welcomed Kenna as she snuggled against him.

His hand played with the ends of her hair as he tried to put his finger on what had occurred. He had never been so worried than when he'd seen Daryn with Kenna. Humans rarely refused Fae. When Kenna had chosen him, his elation had been great, as had his need to leave the clearing and get her somewhere private.

Immediately, he'd thought of his chamber. Of all the times he'd taken a woman, none had ever seen his refuge. Yet, he didn't regret bringing Kenna. It felt right that she was here with him.

As it had felt right taking her again. It seemed when it

came to Kenna, he couldn't think clearly. All he wanted was to be near her.

And that's when he realized what had happened.

He gazed at the stone ceiling and tried to recall the exact moment he had fallen in love with Kenna. His heart melted just thinking of her.

"What are you thinking that has you smiling so?" she asked as she leaned up on an elbow and gazed down at him.

"That I want you again."

"So soon?" she asked with a giggle.

"I always want you."

Her smile faded and she bit her lip, a sign that she was nervous. "Why me?"

"I don't know, and it doesn't matter. It is you."

"You came for me tonight. I didn't expect you to."

Frang pushed her hair behind her ear. "It was always my intention. I'm glad you chose me over Daryn."

"And if I'd have said I wanted both of you?" she teased.

"I'd have agreed, as would have Daryn."

Her amber eyes widened. "Truly?"

"Truly. You don't understand yet the magic of this night, nor the pull the Fae have on humans."

"I understand that pull all too well," she said tightly. "He would have taken me whether I really wanted it or not."

Frang laughed. "Oh, you would have wanted it. Never doubt that."

"But it wouldn't have been you."

He moved her until she straddled him and brought her head down for a kiss. "Why me?" he posed her question back at her.

She smiled. "Because you are everything I've ever wanted in a man. You sacrifice yourself for many, despite the power you have as high priest. Your loyalty to Conall and his clan staggers me. Because you chose to save me instead of taking the book for yourself. Because you are you."

Frang had never been so humbled in his life. "You're an amazing woman, Kenna."

She smiled and shrugged. "I'm simply a woman who has found a man who pleases her."

"Then let me please you some more," he said and lifted her hips until her sex hovered over his rod. "Do you want more?"

"I always want more of you," she whispered.

Frang watched as she slowly lowered herself on his rod. When she was seated fully, he reached up and cupped her breasts. "This position gives a woman complete control."

"Not complete," she said as he ran his fingers over her nipple.

He smiled at the look of pleasure that passed over her face. "Let me show you."

Reluctantly, he released her plump breasts and moved his hands to her hips. With his hands he moved her hips back and forth, then around in circles.

"Oh, my," she said breathlessly. "That feels...wonderful."

Wonderful didn't describe the emotions running rampant in Frang. Through half-closed eyes he watched Kenna brace her hands on his chest and begin to slowly move her hips front to back.

Even after experiencing a climax not five minutes

before, he could feel himself rising to another one quickly. Just watching Kenna was enough to make him come. She had no idea how sensual and erotic she was.

His hands moved from her hips to the indent of her small waist up to her breasts. He couldn't get enough of them, and because he knew how sensitive they were, they brought great pleasure to Kenna.

Softly he ran his fingers over her nipples and watched as her mouth opened on a moan and her head dropped back. Her nipples puckered beneath his fingers

Her tempo increased, and it was all he could do to concentrate and not give in to the need to come. Little cries of pleasure poured from her mouth the more his fingers worked her breasts.

Just when he didn't think he could last much longer, she leaned over him, her red hair falling around them to shut out the outside world and kissed him.

He felt her stiffen and clench around his rod. A heartbeat later, he gripped her hips and plunged deep inside of her until he touched her womb. Only then did he allow the orgasm loose.

As wave upon wave of pleasure engulfed him, Kenna placed kisses on his face, softly calling his name. He wrapped his arms around her and held her against his chest, still deep inside her.

He didn't want to move, didn't want the outside world to interfere in their haven, but there was no stopping the outside world. Not now. Not ever.

With his body sated and his heart full, Frang found himself drifting off to sleep. Kenna shifted and his arms tightened around her.

"I'm not going anywhere," she whispered in his ear.

He let her move off him and snuggle against his side. And with a silent promise to himself to rest for a few hours and enjoy the solitude with Kenna, he allowed sleep to claim him.

* * *

Tears coursed down Kenna's face. Her night with Frang had shown her one important thing—she was in love with him. While he slept, she plotted her departure.

The more she thought about leaving, the more she didn't want to, until there came a time that she knew she had to get up and leave or stay with Frang forever. And she cared too much for him and the other Druids to allow Wallace to kill them.

Slowly, she pulled away from him and slid from the bed. For long moments she stood beside the bed and stared down at him. He was sprawled across the covers, his long hair tousled from their lovemaking.

Even in sleep he looked powerful and magnificent, a force to be reckoned with.

"I love you," she whispered, wishing she'd had the courage to tell him before.

Her hands shook as she reached for her robe now ripped and destroyed and pressed it against her body. Her gaze turned back to Frang, and she couldn't stop herself from reaching over and smoothing back a lock of dark hair that had fallen over his forehead.

And before she could change her mind, she hastened from his chamber. The stone circle was empty as everyone preferred to seek their fulfillment in the forest. Only the moon saw her as she ran to her chamber naked.

Once inside, she tossed aside the ruined robe and reached for her gown. She hastily pulled it on and slipped on new shoes. Then, she turned to the book. She knelt down and pulled out the bag that contained the Book of Magic from beneath her bed.

She hoped Frang would find it and destroy it once she was gone. It had been her plan to throw it in the fire that night, but she hadn't wanted everyone to see her carrying it. And she had been afraid that she might need it.

After making sure she had memorized the spell correctly, she tucked the bag back into its hiding spot and strapped the dagger on her thigh beneath her skirts. She stood and looked around the chamber that had been her home for nearly a week.

"I can do this," she murmured and took a deep, reassuring breath before leaving the chamber.

She let her gaze wander over the inside of the stone circle, the place where the Druids lived, learned and taught the power of their ways. Beyond she could just make out the towers from MacInnes castle. There were so many people she had wanted to say farewell to but couldn't take the chance.

Off to her left the Beltane fire still roared. She turned to her right and left the magical stone circle, silently picking her way through the forest. Several times she came upon people coupling, and it brought a pain to her chest as she thought of Frang.

Moans of desire and cries of rapture filled the night air as Druids, Fae, and humans alike took their pleasure. Her body still hummed with the need Frang had awoken in her, a need she had never felt before him, a need that she would never feel again.

Her feet paused as she thought she heard Malina's voice. She wondered if her new friend had found a Fae to share in her passion that night, and she regretted not being able to hear Malina speak of it in the morning.

She managed to stay undetected and unnoticed by even the Fae. She kept to the shadows and made her way around the clearing. Upon nearing the spot, she was supposed to meet Wallace, she rounded a tree and found herself staring at a couple standing against a tree, the woman's legs wrapped around the man as he pumped furiously inside of her.

Kenna's sex clenched as she wondered how it would feel to have Frang hold her thus. Suddenly, the man's eyes opened, and she found herself staring into swirling blue eyes—Fae eyes. He smiled at her as she continued on, trying her best to forget the image the couple made and the cries of the woman's pleasure as she climaxed.

By the time Kenna reached the spot she was to meet Wallace, her nerves were frazzled. She jumped at every sound wondering if it was her laird or worse, Frang.

For she knew if Frang did appear, she wouldn't be able to lie to him. She'd end up telling him everything, and if the Druids and MacInnes clan were to survive, she had to keep to her plan.

"And here I thought you might be too scared to show up," Wallace said as he rounded a tree and leaned against it.

She gritted her teeth and glared at the man had been her laird. "Aye, I'm here."

"And the book?"

She smiled in the darkness. "Tell me something, Laird, why did you want me as your bride?"

"You were easily controlled, and your knowledge of herbs was useful to me. I had thought to have already made you mine by now, but you fought me at every turn."

"Fought you?"

He laughed and ran a finger down her arm. "Who do you think sent the men to look through your cottage or threaten you in the forest?"

"The Carmichael men?"

"Ah, that was me as well. I just knew you'd come running to me after they were through with you."

"Too bad Frang ruined your plans."

Wallace laughed. "Things have a way of working out to my advantage. Now, where is the book?" he asked, his voice cold and menacing.

"I knew you wouldn't keep your word, so to ensure that you leave everyone here safe and alone, I've hidden it."

He took a threatening step toward her and gripped her arms painfully as he jerked her up on her tiptoes. "Hidden it?" he snarled. "Where?"

"I will tell you only after we've returned to your clan."

"You are a fool," he hissed and pushed her away from him.

Kenna hit a tree with her back then tripped on her feet and fell to her side. She leaned on her elbow and looked up at the Wallace. "Are you afraid I might not keep the bargain?"

He laughed, the sound evil and malicious. "Oh, Kenna. I'm not worried about your bargain at all." He leaned down until his face was inches from hers. "You've only succeeded in determining what my next move will be. For you see, that book is more important than anything to me."

The fear that had threatened to take hold of Kenna all night wrapped its steel manacles firmly around her and refused to let go.

"You cannot kill them all."

"I can do anything I want," he said and pulled her to her feet. "Especially now that I have you."

31

Frang woke and reached for Kenna. When his search came up vacant, his eyes flew open, and he turned his head to find the bed empty.

A frisson of fear wrapped around his heart. With a shaking hand, he rose up on his elbow and felt the spot she had been sleeping to find it cool to the touch. He swallowed past the lump in his throat and leaned forward until his head touched the pillow she had lain on.

He closed his eyes and used his power to find her, praying that she hadn't done the unthinkable and gone to the Wallace by herself.

It didn't take long for him to locate her. He let out a roar of rage as he saw the Wallace dragging her toward his camp. He knew in his heart she was probably gone from him forever, but he refused to let her go without a fight. He jumped from the bed and hurried to put on his kilt and weapons. In two strides he was at his door and threw it open to find Conall with his fist raised as if he were about to knock.

Conall's smile fell as he took in Frang's appearance. "What has happened?"

"Kenna," Frang said as he pushed passed his friend, grabbing his sword as he did. He found Brock and Sampson waiting for him inside the stones. "We have to move quickly. Kenna has gone to the Wallace."

Brock stopped him with a hand on his arm. "Frang. Wallace's soldiers arrived. There are thirty more, bringing his total to fifty."

"I've got many more than that," Conall said as he joined them.

Frang sighed and looked over his shoulder at Conall. "Aye, but your numbers won't mean anything next to his magic. Don't bother mentioning Glenna, for I won't have her putting herself and the baby in harm's way."

"How did you...?" Conall started then stopped. "Frang, you cannot mean to battle this man by yourself."

"It's the only way. I cannot knowingly send men to their deaths."

Sampson stepped forward. "We could gather all the Druids. Collectively their magic is strong."

"The ones that have it, aye," Frang agreed. "But let us not forget this is Beltane. Gathering them would be near impossible."

"Shite," Conall cursed as he raked a hand through his hair. "Let's go then."

"Us?" Frang said then shook his head. "I go alone."

"The hell you do," Conall ground out.

Frang watched as Sampson and Brock moved to stand beside Conall, offering their aid to the laird. "I beg each of you," Frang said softly. "Don't do this."

Conall smiled and gripped his sword. "There's nothing you can do to stop me."

"Or me," said a feminine voice.

They all turned to find Glenna walking toward them. She glared at her husband. "Did you really think I'd let you go into battle without me watching your back?" She tsked and turned to Frang. "And you. What are you thinking, facing this monster alone?"

"Glenna, he knows magic. I don't know how strong he is."

She laughed and linked hands with her husband. "After what we faced for the prophecy, this is nothing. Besides, I'll be safely out of harm's way."

Frang looked to Conall, and when Conall nodded his head, Frang knew there was no turning Glenna back. "Just make sure he doesn't see you."

"He won't," she promised.

Frang had his doubts, but with his emotions in an uproar, he couldn't trust his instincts. He left the stones, the others following close behind him.

* * *

Kenna had known the Wallace would react just as he had. She had counted on it. Now that she was inside his camp, she waited for her chance to use the spell she had memorized.

She winced as his hand tightened around her arm as he dragged her through his camp to an oak where he pushed her down. Kenna caught herself with her hands just before her face slammed into the rough bark of the tree.

Her breath came out in a rush, but before she could turn around, more hands grabbed her and jerked her back against the tree. She bit her lip to keep from crying out as the men pulled her arms back and around the trunk of the tree then tied them.

None of the men would look her in the eye, men she had known her entire life were now treating her as if she were an enemy. And to them, she was. She didn't want to kill them, but if they gave her no other choice, she would do what she had to.

Her eyes wandered the camp taking in everything and everyone. There were at least three dozen armed men at the ready. Waiting. Her gaze moved to find Wallace standing off by himself staring into the forest as if he awaited someone.

She tried to adjust her position and only succeeded in scraping her back with the bark. Kenna sighed as tears pricked her eyes. She refused to let any of them see her cry, so she closed her eyes and immediately thought of Frang. Was he still asleep? Had he woken and found her gone yet? When he did, what would he think?

She leaned her head back against the tree and began to repeat the spell in her head again. She didn't want fear to make her forget the words, for her laird could be most fearsome when he wanted.

A commotion caused her to open her eyes, and what she beheld made her skin crawl in revulsion. Malina stood in Wallace's arms, Kenna's bag draped over her shoulder. When Malina turned and saw her, she smiled at Kenna and shrugged her shoulder as if to say she had no other choice but to take it.

Anger surged through Kenna. She wished she could get up and confront Malina, but no matter how hard she struggled, she only managed to scrap her wrists with the coarse rope.

In the end, it was Malina who came to her.

"You should have known," she said as she stood over Kenna.

Kenna raised her eyes and glared at the woman she had called friend. "How did you know I had it?"

She laughed. "I wouldn't have had Wallace not told me."

"I can't believe you," Kenna spat. "You are a Druid."

"A Druid who has been waiting for five years to be given the high priest position," she screeched. "No one would do it. All waited for Frang to return. They were so sure he would."

"And he did."

Malina rolled her eyes. "He might have, but it isn't the same Frang who's returned. He's different and not fit to lead the Druids."

"But you are?"

"Most certainly, and after tonight, I will."

Kenna shook her head sadly. "If you think that, I feel sorry for you."

"The Wallace promised me I would be leader of the Druids."

Kenna shrugged. "Believe him at your own risk."

"Don't try any of that," Malina warned. "He already told me everything you would say to dissuade me."

Kenna struggled to think of something that would return her friend to the Druid she had been days ago.

"What about the Fae you were looking forward to being with tonight? Did you find him?"

"I don't need a Fae when I had your laird."

Kenna sighed. "You're going to destroy everyone, Malina. Including yourself."

"We'll see about that," Malina said and walked away.

Kenna's gaze found Wallace again, this time he held the Book of Magic and stroked it as if it were a lover. His eyes were closed, and his lips moved as if he were speaking to it. It was then she realized just how foolhardy she had been. Had she really wanted to save everyone, she would have spoken with Frang so they could have attacked together.

"Frang, forgive me," she whispered.

* * *

"Glenna is in place," Conall whispered as they approached Wallace's camp.

Frang nodded and knelt near a clump of ferns. "Good. Brock, Sampson, I want you both to circle the camp and make sure there are no surprises."

The Warriors nodded and moved off to do as ordered.

"We need more than just four men," Conall said. "As much as I'd like to think we could take them on our own, I think we should have brought more."

"I wish we could have. If you think you can find any of your men, by all means, go and get them." Frang looked as Conall sighed and shook his head.

"If only this had happened any other night."

"He planned it this way," Frang said.

Conall rolled his shoulders to loosen them. "I'm ready to get the bastard."

"You'll have your chance."

No sooner were the words out of his mouth than he felt the air stir around him. He turned and found Aimery standing behind him.

"Tread carefully, Frang," Aimery warned. "Wallace has your woman captive. She tried to outwit him, but it didn't work to her advantage."

Frang tried to calm the hatred that rose up in him. "I know."

"You need to attack before he does," Aimery continued. His gaze moved to Conall. "We'll keep Glenna safe, so do not worry about her."

"Have you come to aid us?" Conall asked.

Aimery shook his head. "I can only protect Glenna, but I will be watching. If I can help, I will."

Frang ran a hand down his face. "Kenna."

"She wanted to do this for you," Aimery said. "It might have worked if Malina hadn't brought Wallace the book."

"What?" Conall and Frang whispered together.

Aimery moved closer to them. "Wallace turned Malina. Her mind was easy to peer into, but now that I have, I wish I hadn't. The power she's wanted since you left has grown with each month. She waited patiently for the Druids to make her high priest, and when they didn't, her anger festered."

"Giving Wallace just what he needed when he approached her," Frang finished for him. "Shite. Not only does he have Kenna, but he has the book, giving him more power than I had anticipated."

"He is overconfident."

Frang nodded. "Aimery, can you get everyone that is frolicking in the forest safely to the stones?"

"I will try. Be wary," Aimery cautioned again before he faded from them.

Conall turned his silver eyes to him. "What is your plan now?"

Frang looked over his shoulder at the camp. "We draw him out.

32

When Frang spotted Kenna tied to a tree, he had the overwhelming urge to charge into the camp and kill anyone who had dared to touch her.

"Easy," Conall said as he laid a hand on Frang's shoulder. "We'll get her out."

Frang stood as Brock and Sampson approached. "Did you find anything?" he asked.

They shook their heads. "All is clear," Sampson said.

"Off to the left Wallace stands by himself holding the book. Malina is with him."

"Aye," Frang said. "She's sided with him."

Brock's face showed his disappointment and shock. "Of all the people, I would never have guessed Malina. She never showed any outward signs."

"Those are the people you need to watch the most," Frang said. He glanced at Kenna once more before he turned to the three men. "Glenna will be waiting for our sign. Are you ready?"

The three nodded, and they moved off to take their

positions. Frang glanced around the forest. He focused inside of himself and found the calm he would need to face Wallace, for only a serene man would win against one such as Wallace.

When he was ready, he stepped out from behind a tree and faced the camp. It didn't take long for someone to spot him as men yelled for Wallace and scrambled to get their weapons.

Wallace slowly walked toward him, an arrogant smile on his lips. "I wondered when you would show up. I've a great need to see your head detached from your body."

"Why don't you come out and get it?"

Wallace laughed. "I think I would much prefer you to come to me."

"If you are as powerful as you think you are, you have no need for your shield around your camp."

"You don't know the meaning of powerful," Wallace taunted. "I could show you more power than you ever dreamt of."

Frang laughed. "Just because you have the book?"

"Because I have the book. I have in my possession something men have searched centuries for."

"Power can be a heady thing. Did you know that each time you use a spell from the book, a piece of your soul is destroyed?"

Wallace laughed. "A nice try, Frang, but I know better."

"Do you now?"

"I know everything."

Frang unsheathed his sword. "Then you'll know that I've come for Kenna. And the book."

"You'll never succeed."

"A wise woman once told me to never to say never," he said as he raised his sword.

Wallace's eyes flashed with anger an instant before his mouth began to move and a ball of lightning formed in his hand. Frang didn't have time to blink before Wallace threw the lightning ball at him.

Frang flew backwards as it surrounded him and struck pain throughout his body with each strike. He took a deep breath and tried to pull the lightning away from him. But the more he pulled, the faster the lightning struck him, numbing all his muscles so he couldn't move them.

Desperately, he shifted through his mind trying to find a calm place and push aside the pain. Only then was he able to pull the lightning from him, once more forming the ball. For a moment he thought about tossing it back at Wallace, but what if Wallace moved and it hit Kenna instead.

So, Frang smashed it into the earth, dissolving the spell instantly. He reached for his sword and rose to his feet. Wallace's eyes grew round as he saw Frang approach him.

"So, you know some magic?"

Frang shrugged. "You could say that."

"I've wanted to test myself. Now, you've given me the chance."

"Then come and get me."

Frang smiled as Wallace let down the shield around the camp and walked into the forest. Frang raised his sword, ready for an attack. The light of the moon reflected off the blade, illuminating the Fae markings.

He moved his gaze back to the Wallace and waited.

Instead of another spell, Wallace raised his hand and Callum moved toward him.

Frang took a deep breath and watched as Wallace's first in command came at him.

"I knew I'd have a chance to kill you," Callum boasted.

They began to circle each other, each measuring his opponent.

"It's not good to brag before you have something to brag about," Frang said.

"Oh, I have no doubt I'll kill you."

Frang stepped to the side as Callum lunged, and Frang used that advantage to spin and come up behind Callum. With the tip of his sword, he sliced Callum from shoulder to waist.

Callum hissed and jerked away. He touched his wound and looked at the blood on his fingers. "No one draws my blood and lives."

"Then come and get me," Frang taunted.

Callum was large and his arms longer, but Frang used his speed and wit to stay out of reach of Callum's sword. It wasn't long before the big man began to tire. When Callum lunged toward him, Frang pivoted and drove his sword into Callum's chest.

Frang pushed Callum's dead body to the ground and withdrew his sword to face Wallace. "Is that the best you can do?"

Wallace raised his hand and twenty-five of his soldiers ran at Frang.

In a heartbeat, fire sprang around them, stopping the soldiers from reaching him. He looked out over the tall flames to find Wallace glowering at him.

Frang moved away from the screaming men. Inside Wallace's camp he saw Conall, Brock and Sampson fighting the other half of Wallace's men, and every so often out of the corner of his eye he saw a bolt of fire shoot from high atop the cliff toward the soldiers fighting Conall.

"No matter what you do, you won't win against me," Wallace said as he advanced on Frang.

Frang shrugged. "'Tis you who are mistaken. You've let the power of those spells blind you to what is all around you."

"The Druids?" Wallace laughed. "They worship nature and heal. They've no real power."

Frang just smiled, letting Wallace believe what he wanted. He rotated his wrist, his sword swirling around him. And just before he was going to attack, Wallace disappeared.

Frang didn't budge. The sounds of the men's screams were too loud for him to ignore as he listened for Wallace's approach. It was the movement of air around him that let him know where Wallace was.

Frang lowered his sword so that the tip faced the ground, and he held the hilt with both hands. He stepped back the same time he shoved his blade backwards. There was a grunt as sword meet flesh. He pulled his sword free and turned to find Wallace clutching his side.

"How did you know?" Wallace grunted.

"I'm a Druid, that's how." He glanced at Kenna to find men fighting around her, and with her being bound, she had nowhere to go. It was only a matter of time before she was wounded.

Without hesitation, Frang kicked Wallace in the face.

Wallace grunted as blood poured from his nose and he fell onto his back. Frang had precious little time. He quickly moved into the camp and rushed toward Kenna.

"I'm sorry," she said as soon as he approached.

He shook his head as he cut her bonds loose. "Let's get out of here first then you can apologize and tell me why you didn't trust me."

She took his hand as he helped her to her feet. "Frang."

"Not now," he hissed. He dragged her to the edge of the camp. "Go to the stones. Aimery is gathering everyone in there. The Fae will keep you safe."

She hesitated as she looked at him. "And you?"

"I'll come as soon as..."

* * *

Kenna gasped as Frang was thrown backwards and pinned against a tree. His entire body shook with pain as lightning struck him again and again. She took a step toward him as he valiantly tried to pull the lightning from him.

She couldn't imagine the pain he felt. With her heart hammering in her ears, she ran to him. Only to halt as another ball of lightning soon joined the first.

Kenna turned to find Wallace about twenty strides from Frang, a smile of pure malice on his face as his lips moved in another spell.

Frustration gripped Kenna as she realized how helpless she was against Wallace and his spells. Then she remembered a spell she had found as she'd looked through the book. She pivoted and rushed to where she had seen Wallace put the book.

She was nearly there when something gripped her hair and yanked. Hard.

Kenna fell to her back, knocking the breath from her body. She gasped and clawed at the earth while she struggled to breathe. Finally, her lungs filled with precious air.

She turned over onto her hands and knees and slowly rose. Standing between her and the book was Malina. "Get out of my way."

"I'll kill you first," Malina hissed.

Kenna smiled. "You can try, but I am going to get that book." Behind her she could hear Frang bite back screams of pain. It was love, and pure willpower, that drove her toward Malina.

Before the tall priestess could raise her arms, Kenna used all her strength to backhand her. When Malina doubled over clutching her face, Kenna knew she had to finish it. She punched Malina in the stomach, and she fell to the ground, unmoving.

Kenna gripped her hand as pain traveled through her hand and up her arm. She moved to the book and flipped it open, desperately searching for the spell. Every now and again she would glance at Frang. His strength was rapidly waning, and it wouldn't be long before Wallace killed him.

She might not be able to kill Wallace herself, but she could sure make the fight between him and Frang fair. She flipped through more pages and spotted the one she needed. She opened her mouth to say the words when a man, nay a Fae, suddenly appeared in front of her.

"Don't," he warned.

Kenna looked from his swirling blue eyes to Frang then back to the Fae. "I have to."

"You will lose part of your soul."

She smiled. "It's worth it."

When he didn't say more, she bent her head and proceeded to say the spell aloud.

"The gods of the earth, hear me now as I call upon you. Heat of fire, heat of light, end Wallace's voice before my sight."

As soon as the last word left her mouth, the spell Wallace had been speaking stopped, though his lips continued to move. Kenna rose as his gaze swung to hers.

"The spells only work if you speak them," she stated triumphantly.

Wallace threw back his head and howled, though no sound came from his throat. Kenna rushed to Frang, who could barely lift his head.

She reached for him and lightning struck her. She screamed as her flesh was scorched. All her efforts to stop Wallace had been in vain if she couldn't free Frang.

"Use his sword," the Fae whispered in her head.

Kenna turned to him and watched as his eyes moved beyond her. She turned and found Frang's sword lying on the ground. She rushed to it and lifted the heavy weapon in her hand. It took both hands to hold it as she hurried back to Frang, and it took all her strength to lift it when she reached him.

"I love you," she screamed as she struck the lightning surrounding Frang, all the while praying the blade didn't touch him.

Instantly the lightning disappeared and Frang

crumpled to the ground. Kenna dropped his sword and fell to her knees beside him. She smoothed back his hair from his sweat soaked forehead and felt the tears begin to fall.

"I was too late," she whispered.

She reached for Frang's hand when someone grabbed her from behind and hauled her up. She turned to find Wallace sneering at her. She didn't need to hear his words to know he meant to kill her.

Her gaze moved around the camp, the men that had come with Frang had killed most of Wallace's men, though they still fought a few. And the Fae, he had left them.

There was only her, Wallace, and Frang.

Her eyes moved to Frang. Her only regret was not telling him she loved him sooner. The arm around her throat tightened as it was joined by the feel of something cool and hard...a dagger.

She didn't fight Wallace as he dragged her toward the book, kicking Malina out of the way. He pointed at the book with the dagger, but Kenna only shook her head.

"You're going to kill me anyway, so I'd rather die knowing you won't ever be able to use any of the spells again."

The blade pricked her throat and she felt something warm and sticky roll down her chest. But she never wavered.

"Conall and the Druids will beat your men then they will destroy the book as it should have been destroyed years ago."

The blade pressed deeper into her skin, and she knew it was the end. She didn't care anymore, not if Frang was gone. She closed her eyes and accepted her fate.

And just as she expected to feel the dagger slice open her throat, Wallace's hand slowly fell away. She heard a thump and looked down to find Wallace on the ground with his eyes staring at nothing.

It was then she saw Frang's sword. She whirled around and saw him standing, his hand against a tree to keep his balance.

"Frang," she called as she ran to him.

He enfolded her in his arms as they fell to their knees. She touched his face, kissing him between her tears. "I thought I had lost you."

"You nearly did," he rasped.

She took in a shaky breath. "You came for me."

He smiled as he cupped her face in his hands. "I would have died for you."

She melted against him as he took her mouth in a searing kiss, one that told her there was much more pleasure to come. When he broke the kiss, she gripped his shoulders and struggled to get her desire back under control.

"Did I hear you right?" he asked.

She blinked up at him. "What?"

"Did you say you loved me?"

She laughed and flung her arms around his neck. "Aye, Frang Malcolm. I love you."

His arms held her tightly. "'Tis a good thing since I love you."

Her heart skipped a beat. She slowly pulled out of his embrace to look into his bright blue eyes. "You do?"

"For quite some time," he confessed. "I don't know how I survived three hundred years without you, Kenna, but I don't want to go another day without you by my side. Be my wife, and I'll give you as many children as you want."

Tears blurred her vision. "You're giving me the world, and I'm giving you nothing."

"You're giving me your heart. That is more than enough."

Kenna nodded as words eluded her. Frang laughed and kissed her again.

It was then she noticed how quiet the forest had become. When Frang ended the kiss, they both looked over to find Conall and two other men watching them with knowing smiles on their faces.

"She's going to be my wife," Frang announced.

Conall laughed. "We heard. Now, let's get you both back to the stones so we can see to your injuries."

Kenna managed to support Frang as he slowly got to his feet, but it took Conall's aide to get him to the stones. They passed a burnt circle on the forest floor, which made Kenna look around her.

"Where are Wallace's men?"

"The ones that aren't dead ran off as soon as Glenna stopped the fire," Conall said. "I don't think we'll be seeing them again."

No other words were spoken until they reached the stones. Frang was laid out on one of the long, flat stones. Kenna turned to get her herbs when the Fae she had seen at Wallace's camp moved behind her.

"Aimery, let her through," Frang whispered.

Kenna glanced at Frang and knew he was weakening by the moment. She turned back to Aimery. "Please let me pass. I must save him."

"That is for me to do." The Fae stepped around her.

Kenna didn't fight when Conall pulled her to Frang's other side.

"Watch," he whispered in her ear before he moved away.

Kenna's eyes widened as Aimery held his hands palm down over Frang and closed his eyes. Instantly, the shallow pallor of Frang's skin improved, the burn marks from the lightning vanished and light surrounded him.

Then, Aimery stepped back and Frang opened his eyes. He smiled up at Aimery.

"Thank you."

Aimery laughed and held out a hand to help Frang sit up. "You are most welcome."

Kenna's heart accelerated as Frang turned to her. He reached out his arms for her, and it was all the encouragement she needed. She buried her face in his neck and breathed in the scent that was his alone.

When she looked into his eyes she saw a future filled with pleasure and happiness and magic. She had been given her most treasured fantasy, and she intended to make sure she enjoyed every moment of it.

* * *

Frang stared down at the Book of Magic. The part of the forest Wallace had used for his camp had been cleared of the dead, and Malina, their traitor, had been dealt with swiftly.

Aimery had wiped her memories of Druids and Fae and put her in a village on the other side of Scotland. She would not bother them again, but evil would always find its way to the Glen.

He took a deep breath as the center of the stone in the book began to glow red. The book knew when something powerful was near, and it called to them.

Yet, Aimery was strong enough not to heed that call, for if he touched the book, it would kill him.

"What are you waiting on?" Frang asked as he came to stand beside him.

Aimery shrugged. "So much power in one book."

"Aye, that's the truth. I'll feel much better about it once it's gone."

Aimery didn't hesitate. He extended his hand to the book and it erupted in flames. They stood and watched until there was nothing left but ashes.

"Let me," Frang said as he motioned his hand up and the ashes followed into the air. With no more than a flick of his wrist, Frang scattered the ashes to the wind.

"Thank you."

Frang shook his head. "Nay, thank you. We wouldn't have succeeded without you. You saved all of us."

Aimery smiled and shifted his gaze over Frang's shoulder where Kenna awaited him. "Someone is waiting for you."

Frang looked over his shoulder and waved to Kenna. "I hope to see you soon," he said to Aimery.

The Fae smiled as Frang moved to join Kenna. Once they were gone, he whispered, "You'll see me sooner than you think."

EPILOGUE

Frang sighed and shifted his shoulders again.

"She'll be here," Conall said for the hundredth time that morning.

Frang was nervous. He was never nervous, but it was his wedding day, and he feared that Kenna would change her mind. And after their conversation with Aimery the night before, he wouldn't blame her.

Because of his service to the Druids and the Fae, King Theron and Queen Rufina were gifting him and Kenna with immortality if they so wanted it. They had also asked that Frang stay as High Priest at the Druid's Glen.

Neither he nor Kenna had decide on either offer. Now, as he stood atop the cliff overlooking the forest, loch and MacInnes castle, he wondered how he could have ever left such a magical, beautiful place.

He turned then and spotted Kenna walking toward him, a bright smile on her face. Her beautiful flame hair was down with a circle of white and yellow flowers adorning her head. Her gown was of the palest yellow and unadorned in any way except for the Malcolm plaid that was draped from one shoulder to her hip then up her back and pinned together.

The ceremony was a traditional Druid ceremony, one that lasted far longer than he would have liked since all he wanted was be alone with Kenna and kiss every inch of her luscious skin.

Yet, in a heartbeat, it was over, and Kenna was well and truly his.

"Do you regret it?" she asked.

"Never," he replied as he bent down to claim her lips.

Through all the good wishes, Frang saw Aimery standing off to the side, waiting for their decisions. Finally, everyone but Conall and Glenna had moved to the castle for the celebration.

It was then Aimery stepped forward. "I'm very happy for you both."

"Even though you didn't want me to read from the book?" Kenna asked.

Aimery smiled. "I was testing you."

"Thank you," Frang said. "Thank you for everything."

Aimery shrugged. "It was you we have to thank. You and Kenna, for without the bravery each of you displayed, none of us would be standing here now."

"I second that," Conall said.

Frang wrapped an arm around Kenna's waist and pulled her against his side. He knew what Aimery was waiting on. "Are you ready to make a decision?"

She nodded. "I am."

"Then what are they?" Aimery asked.

"We'll stay with the Druids," Frang said. "But not

forever. I think it is good for them to have a new high priest."

"So, you aren't going to take the gift of immortality?" Aimery asked, his brow furrowed.

"We didn't say that," Kenna said.

Aimery glanced from one to the other. "So, you are?"

Frang and Kenna looked at each other. "We didn't say that either."

"Are you going to give me an answer on that?" Aimery asked.

Frang looked into Kenna's amber eyes and shook his head. "That gift is one we will let the Fae decide upon."

Aimery smiled. "A wise choice."

"Now," Frang said as he scooped Kenna up in his arms, "I'm going to take my wife to my chamber and make love to her the rest of the day."

"I thought I'd come down and talk with you about the defense of the forest," Conall yelled as they walked away.

"Do it and die," Kenna shouted as she smiled back at him.

Frang smiled at his new wife. "I don't know what the future holds for us. Throughout time the Glen has been a place where many battles have been fought against evil."

"None of that matters as long as I'm with you. We have love and magic on our side, Frang. What else could we ask for?"

He winked at her. "Children?"

She laughed. "As you said, you never know what the future holds."

Thank you for reading **HIGHLAND MAGIC**.
Want to know what happens next in the series?
Order **MYSTIC TRINITY** right now!

As Commander of the Fae army, Aimery is used to tracking evil and putting an end to it. When one of the rare and treasured blue dragons is killed and an egg stolen, Aimery is ordered to find the murderer. He never expects it to be one of his closest friends...

Kyndra is a priestess of the Dragon Order sworn to protect all dragons in the Realm of the Fae. She is sent by the high priestess to accompany Aimery and return the killer for execution. Aimery is instantly drawn to the sword-wielding priestess, but he knows he cannot have Kyndra. Her life is sworn to the dragons, to be touched by no man. Neither expects to find desire and unyielding passion in the other. Yet when they track the killer to another realm, Aimery's life is at stake and Kyndra gives herself to him and the love she cannot deny in order to save him...

MYSTIC TRINITY IS NOW AVAILABLE!

Donna Grant
www.DonnaGrant.com
www.MotherofDragonsBooks.com

NEVER MISS A NEW BOOK FROM DONNA GRANT!

Sign up for Donna's email newsletter at www.DonnaGrant.com

Be the first to get notified of new releases and be eligible for special subscribers-only exclusive content and giveaways. Sign up today!

ABOUT THE AUTHOR

New York Times and *USA Today* bestselling author Donna Grant has been praised for her "totally addictive" and "unique and sensual" stories. She's written more than one hundred novels spanning multiple genres of romance including the bestselling Dark King series that features a thrilling combination of Dragon Kings, Druids, Fae, and immortal Highlanders who are dark, dangerous, and irresistible. She lives in Texas with her dog and a cat.

Connect with Donna online:
www.DonnaGrant.com
www.MotherofDragonsBooks.com

facebook.com/AuthorDonnaGrant
instagram.com/dgauthor
bookbub.com/authors/donna-grant
goodreads.com/donna_grant
pinterest.com/donnagrant1

www.ingramcontent.com/pod-product-compliance
Lightning Source LLC
La Vergne TN
LVHW030917080826
845145LV00013B/2943

* 9 7 8 1 9 4 2 0 1 7 3 1 8 *